No One Was Watching

Annie Horner

No One Was Watching

No One Was Watching
ISBN 978 1 76041 641 6
Copyright © text Annie Horner 2018
Cover image: Vergessen, by alexandersw

First published 2018 by
GINNINDERRA PRESS
PO Box 3461 Port Adelaide 5015
www.ginninderrapress.com.au

Contents

Foreword

Although I have met a number of people who endured living in out-of-home 'care' during part or all of their childhood, I have not experienced such a childhood. These stories do not intend to speak for these individuals but instead to provide an alternative, imaginative entrée into this once-hidden Australian history. Hence, this is a work of fiction and, although informed by factual events, all the characters and their encounters are my invention.

The work is a creative response to a seminal Senate report of 2004 entitled *Forgotten Australians*. Just as earlier reports had revealed serious abuses perpetrated against Indigenous children (*Bringing Them Home* report, 1997) and the unaccompanied children sent as migrants from Britain and Malta (*Lost Innocence* report, 2001), this report found that the same types of violations were committed against institutionalised Australian-born, non-Indigenous children. The men and women who experienced such childhoods self-identify as 'forgotten Australians', 'care-leavers', 'care-survivors', 'Homies' or 'Wardies'.

The citations which open each story come from Boxall, H., Tomison, A.M., & Hulme, S. (2014), *Historical review of sexual offence and child abuse legislation in Australia: 1788–2013*, Canberra, ACT, Australian Institute of Criminology (http://www.aic.gov.au); McLucas, J. (2004), *Forgotten Australians: A Report on Australians Who Experienced Institutional or Out-of-home Care as Children* (http://www.aph.gov.au//media/ wopapub/senate/committee/clac_ctte/compted_inquiries/2004_07/ inst care/report) National Museum of Australia, (2013); *Inside: Life in Children's Homes and Institutions* (http://www.nam.gov.au/exhibitions/ Inside); Townsend, H. (1988), *Baby boomers: Growing up in Australia in the 1940s, 50s and 60s*, Brookvale, NSW, Simon Schuster.

List of Characters

Amber (1990–) A young woman who rails against hypocrisy and superficial bullshit.

Belinda (1952–) A doll with rosebud lips and an amazing memory.

Bev (1954–) and Dave (1952–) Amber's next-door neighbours. Bev is a care-survivor.

Billy Marshall (1946–) Janet's older brother and care-survivor who watches life from the margins.

Diane (1945–2005) Sharon's sometime friend.

Diedre Taylor-Brown (1910–1964) A good sort who works tirelessly for charity.

Georgie (2011–2017) A little girl who likes to chat with old Billy.

Gladys White (1907–1969) Walter's wife and Victor's mum.

Janet Thomas (née Marshall) (1949–) Our protagonist, who is a care-survivor and woman of extraordinary courage, resilience and hope.

Kaz (1989–) Amber's one-time boyfriend.

Mary Susan Marshall (1920–1954) Janet's mother.

Matron aka Margaret Goodman (1920–2015) A trained nurse and lover of classical music.

Reginald Thomas (1948–2012) A care-survivor and Janet's soulmate.

Robert (Bob) James Marshall (1920–1955) Janet's father.

Robert (1945–) Wendy-Ann's husband.

Sharon (1945–2010) A kid at the same school as Janet and Billy.

Steve (1980–) and Alice (1982–) Georgie's mum and dad.

Susie Marshall (1951–1954) A care-statistic and ghost. Janet's younger sister.

Teddy Taylor-Brown (1905–1970) Diedre's marvellous husband.

Tim (1918–1946) A larrikin who once made Margaret laugh.

Victor White (1925–2005) A timid man and paedophile.

Walter Thomas White (1904–1960). A returned World War I soldier,
    a fitter and turner and the father of Victor.

Wendy-Ann (1948–) A care-survivor and bag lady.

Prologue

'[There are] stories from a number of former residents over
suspicious deaths and burials in unmarked graves.'
Forgotten Australians

There are lots of us little kids down here. Some of us have got straighter bones than others. The crooked ones are usually boys.

This is a world without angst, or pain, or fear. Once we've crossed over, we are becalmed on a clear, horizon-less ocean. A vista that opens onto eternity. Even with dirt clogging our ears and our eyes, we hear and we see.

Everything.

My metamorphosis came about because I was sick. I was ignored. I cried. I was punished. I died. I was committed to the earth. Now here I am in an unmarked grave behind the laundry. I was only three years old but my sensibilities blossomed to full maturity before my dehydrated body had grown cold. This all-seeing, all-knowing capacity situates me as an omniscient narrator. I am able to pluck words from the past, present or future. The difficulty for those still living is finding words. Words from their past that those in the present can hear and those in the future will remember.

My name is Susie and when I was alive I came to live here with my sister Janet and my brother Billy. Janet was five. She was clever. My brother was eight. He wasn't so clever, but he was funny. They never told their stories to anyone. Even if they had, who would have believed them?

That's why I would like to tell them. So you know what really happened. It would provide a sense of cohesion to otherwise dislocated tales. I even thought it might make a wonderful fairy story. I would unmask villains. Rescue victims. Create a unified plot with points of tension, moments of conflict and close with a satisfying resolution. A simple rendering full of hope and redemption.

But, lives broken into fragments refuse to be contained. The shards escape tidy telling. Voices, long silenced, begin to mutter, even shriek. No one agrees on any one narrative. There are no neat endings. The muddled stories make you rage. And gasp. And cringe. And cry.

I will have to remain silent as corpses should and just listen with you. To the cacophony of voices attempting to say the unsayable.

A New Kitchen

'A number of Churches and religious Orders entered into settlements as a result of the commencement of legal action by victims.'
Forgotten Australians

'Jesus, Kaz. This is a shitty part of town. Can't we find something more upmarket?'

'Sure, babe. I'm cool with being a kept man. Neat apartment. Jacuzzi. Massive flat screen. Man cave. Got a sugar daddy hanging around to foot the bill?'

'Ha ha. Well, I s'pose we can fix it up. Wonder if the landlord would let us paint some life into the place. These beige walls do my head in.'

Amber and Kaz move in. Living on Austudy, the choices are limited. The landlord agrees to them painting and never comes back for house inspections. It's an old house, block value only. He doesn't care much as long as they pay the rent and don't set up a some sort of drug lab. Life's pretty sweet. Bit of part-time work, uni, summer on the beach, good friends to share a drink and some laughs.

They've been there nearly two years. They keep to themselves. The neighbours are kind of ordinary but okay. Mostly older couples. They wave hello. That's enough. What does give Kaz the shits is the weekend morning routine. Bloody lawnmowers and leaf-blowers first thing, then the grandkids screaming and yelling out in the backyard. By noon, when he staggers out onto the back veranda with a strong coffee, the air is full of righteous activity. Kaz is pretty laid-back but he hates this morning vibe. In his perfect world, he's kicking back on the veranda of a beach shack, watching a great break and hearing nothing but an occasional magpie. The great Aussie outdoor dream.

Amber scoffs. He can be full of bullshit sometimes.

The couple next door is harmless enough. Early sixties maybe, but not in good shape. Both obese. Big guts and her with massive, swollen legs. She wears leggings. Huge fat sausages straining to burst out of their casings. How she could even think that it was a good look Amber can't imagine.

The wife's name is Bev and she's asked Amber in for a cuppa on several occasions but Amber's pretty busy. Not that Amber is a snob but she wouldn't have a clue what they could talk about.

Bev and Dave have lived there since they were married.

'Been here forty-three years all up. Housing Commission back then but we've finally paid it off. Dave said we might get a caravan soon so we can go up north. It's the fishing he loves. He's happy just sitting in a tinny with a line and some beers.' Bev can share a lot in the short distance from her letter box to the front door.

Dave still works at the abattoir. He's a supervisor now.

'Thank God for that,' says Bev. 'All those years of stinking, blood-spattered overalls. Used to turn my stomach, specially when I was expecting.'

Amber commiserates although she has no experience of abattoirs, bloody overalls or pregnancy. And she certainly has never envisaged herself living in welfare housing.

Over the last couple of weeks, there's been activity next door. Tradies' vans coming and going. A skip on the front kerb. Power tools screaming.

Amber sees Bev at the letter box.

'Getting a new kitchen fitted out. Waited all my life for a decent stove and we're even getting a dishwasher. Tell you, luv, I never saw myself having something so flash. Come and have a look when it's finished.'

A week later, Bev is beaming as she shows Amber through the pokey hallway and into her dazzling new kitchen. 'Could never have got it without the payout, you know.'

'Oh. What sort of payout?' Amber is only half interested.

'For the abuse. When I was a kid in a home.'

Amber just stares. She breathes out slowly as she takes it all in. The gleaming stainless steel, the stone bench top, the multifunction taps, the pristine white cabinet work, the matte-finished splashback, the timber clip flooring and the latest model stove with multiple burners and a double oven.

Never Talk to Strangers

'For many people the traumas of a childhood in care did not appreciably resurface and have their fullest impact until mid-life… Flashbacks and vivid recollections of events from childhood grow stronger with age.'
Forgotten Australians

'What's your name?'

'Sue. I'm your daughter.'

She scowls into the daughter's face, peering closer but finding nothing familiar. Confused, she flops back into the recliner. 'I don't remember any Sue,' she mutters. She holds the thought momentarily. 'I don't even like that name so why would I call you Sue?'

'Well, Mum, it's Susan. You called me Susan Ann.'

'That's not the same thing then, is it? It's not Sue.'

'So you do remember me – Susan Ann?'

'I didn't say that. Get that kind lady to come back. I don't know who you are. I want to talk to that other lady.'

Her eyes dart around the room searching for a way through this perpetual haze. Evidence that connects the disappearing dots is displayed on the dressing table. Aluminium-framed photos of Susan and her sister Patricia. Photos of her three grandchildren. And the centrepiece, an embossed silver-framed photo of her late husband. Her Reg. It's five years now since he went.

Sue arranges the daffodils she's brought in, pecks her mother's resistant cheek and leaves.

The kind lady returns and tidies the dressing table. Janet's mind seems to have briefly cleared and her face becomes beatific. She likes this carer. She always has time for a chat.

'Is this a photo of your husband, pet?'

'Yes. That's my Reg. He's gone now.'

Debbie (that's her name) sits on the visitor's chair and Janet remembers.

'It was cancer.' As Janet breathes out, the sigh plumbs her very essence. 'He was my soulmate, you know.'

The jammed doors in Janet's mind swing open and she wanders down the corridors of a more recent past. A past that still contains Reg.

She explains how she'd always seen them as one sturdy tree, gnarly around the trunk and able to withstand the storms of life. And there'd been a few. Like the accident Reg had at work. Fell off a roof and broke both his legs. Couldn't work again for six months. Luckily she had the cleaning job and with the insurance they kept up the house payments.

'Then there was our dear little Susan Ann. We nearly lost her, you know.' She describes how it had happened.

She'd been hit by a car when she got off the school bus. She was only eight and to see her little body connected to tubes and monitors week after week was the worst thing any parent could experience. She and Reg had sat by the bed, their hands soldered together channelling strength and hope. Susan was left with a slight limp but otherwise you'd never know how close to death she'd been. The girls were their pride and joy. Janet and Reg had worked out between them what a strong family might look like, how loving parents might behave. The blueprint they created had proved a success.

'And standing up to that monster in court. I could never have done it without my Reg.'

Debbie pats Janet's arm as the memories of that nightmarish day bring tears that splash into her tea cup.

'You're so lucky to have had such a good man, Janet. Always remember that,' she says.

But it doesn't console. Janet suddenly feels frightened and adrift in a world without Reg.

'And to have your lovely daughters visit.'

Janet's befuddled gaze wanders over the photos then back to the window. When her eyes return to Debbie, there is no one behind the blank stare. Despite the fond recollections of only a moment ago, her children are once again lost to her.

'I don't have any daughters. But my son visits me. He's a lovely boy.'

Debbie smiles. Clears the morning tea things and settles Janet into her recliner. She patiently reminds Janet about her family. 'You have two daughters, Janet. Their names are Sue and Pat. You haven't got a son, but you do have three beautiful little grandchildren: Amber, Brett and Sally. These are their photos.'

The doors in the attic of Janet's mind have swung firmly shut and she stares at the photos, looking for clues and connections. 'When will Reg be back? His dinner will be cold if he's not back soon,' she wails.

Her fingers begin to pluck at the bed cover, at her clothing. Her body becomes rigid. Her eyes dart around a room that is now her only world.

Debbie leaves quietly. She can't bear to remind Janet that Reg is dead. Again. The grief is too awful to witness. A keening soul, too terrible to hear.

'I haven't had my cup of tea yet.'

It's the same every morning after breakfast as she is steered her back to her room.

'Yes, Janet. You've just finished your breakfast and you had your cup of tea.'

'Are you sure? I don't remember that.' She is grumpy and not at all cooperative about changing her saturated pants.

'I think it's time for the continence nurse to have another little chat, Janet.' The voice is already weary despite the fact that it is only eight a.m.

It's a struggle but eventually with clean, dry pants she is settled into her recliner with the TV remote in her hand.

'You see what you can find to watch until morning tea time. This is the volume button here, dear. Just ring your bell if you need anything.'

She does ring the bell. Five times before morning tea time. After the third time, it is ignored.

Janet's days refuse to remain in the present. Time disintegrates unravelling in multicoloured threads as she returns to places and people from her childhood. Long-ago, locked-away memories bubble through the muddle of her mind.

She is back at a big house and a fat lady in a dark blue uniform is twisting her hand as she drags her along to a bed covered with a horrible grey blanket. The corners are tucked in tightly. Everywhere she looks there are more beds just the same. The fat lady orders her to stay where she is until the lunch bell. Janet's face is wet and sticky and her pants are soggy and cold. Dust motes are dancing and swirling colours are everywhere. There are warm blue egg shapes that she can pick up and nurse in her hands. Her mummy is calling and Janet can smell the special perfume she wears when she is going out. The rows and rows of beds fade as Janet moves through the dazzling light in the doorway. Her pants are soft and dry and her shoes don't even whisper as they cross the shiny wooden floor. Her mummy tells her that they will be home soon and Janet can have a Fanta.

'Good morning, Janet. Let's get you changed before you have lunch, shall we?' The carer's voice is soothing.

But Janet resists and starts to scream. She is back in a big bathroom with white, white tiles. There are so many and they sparkle as if they might be a whole sky full of stars. Her mummy has disappeared.

'Take off your clothes,' commands a cross voice.

She is cold and shaky but the lady with the horrible voice grabs her clothes and yanks them off and says that she smells disgusting and her yellow hair ribbons are on the floor and a big pair of scissors chop off her plaits and stingy, smelly stuff is all over her head.

'Get in the bath,' the voice is shouting over her wailing.

Her legs feel like fire despite the cold water and the hairbrush smacks and smacks because she is a naughty girl who won't stop shivering and crying.

The carer battles to disengage Janet from her sodden slacks. Even her socks and sneakers need changing.

'Come on, Janet. Let's get you into some dry clothes,' says a gentle voice not at all like the one that is still playing in Janet's head.

A hateful, nasty voice ordering her to stand in the corner with the wet sheet over her head. Her legs are still throbbing as she disappears from the shouts. She whispers to her shadowy mummy about the sunshine and the rose bush at home with the tiny, tiny, pink buds and lily of the valley perfume overpowers the stink of pee and she smiles but her cheeks are still wet from tears and snot that just run out of her eyes and nose like taps and she shakes and blubbers until she vomits and gets another belting for messing up the shiny floor.

The screaming is incessant and none of the staff can calm her.

'We can't have her disturbing the other clients. I'll get the doctor to prescribe something,' says the duty nurse.

The medication makes her dozy but she remains in the dormitory of her childhood. Her legs are burning and the wooden hairbrush is still beating against her calves and skinny thighs that stick out from under the wet bed sheet shrouding her head. Matron belts her again with a strap this time because she is a dirty, insolent girl, who won't stop wetting the bed.

It's a larger dose and it finally pushes Janet out of the dormitory and into a deep dreamless sleep. The carer sighs as she tidies up the dishevelled bedclothes and lowers the blind.

A new morning and the daughter reads her mother's notes.

Behaviour becoming increasingly difficult. Family consultation recommended.

'Hello, Mum. Did you have a good night?'

'I don't think I know you. And Mummy says that I should never talk to strangers.'

'I'm not a stranger. I'm Susan Ann. You're *my* mummy.'

But Janet has departed. She is somewhere else. In another place and time and has no interest in sharing that with someone called Susan Ann.

The consultation is as expected. Awful. Both the daughters listen to the medical team explaining how their once strong, courageous mother continues to evaporate leaving a frightened cowering child in her place. We are aware that Janet suffered childhood trauma, they say. They also suggest that she may be reliving many of those experiences. The effects of trauma can be lifelong, they believe. Comfort and distraction are the best strategies. Medication gives some respite but they try to keep that to a minimum. They are doing their best. The daughters understand that.

Janet now spends more time in the new courtyard. She is calmer, the staff report. The sisters follow the paved walkway looking for their mother. They pass a woman treadling at an old sewing machine. There is no needle or thread but she is concentrating hard and humming to herself as she pushes a scrap of fabric under the foot. Another is turning the handle of an old wringer. She is busy doing what took her most of every Monday sixty years ago. She must keep going; there's the starching to be done yet. Behind a screen of lavender bushes, Janet is chatting conversationally as she rearranges the tea set on a tray. She lifts the cup and holds it to the rosebud lips of a doll with yellow hair.

Soulmates

'I can't get some of the terrible things he did to me out of my head,
they loom in the shadows of my life and haunt me. This man took
my virginity, my innocence, my development, my potential.'
Forgotten Australians

1

He'd never said anything before they were married. Maybe he couldn't
find the words. In his experience, words could be as difficult to grasp
as the eels he sometimes hooked off the jetty on Saturday afternoons.

But she remembers how jittery he was on their wedding night. His
usual quiet and reassuring demeanour seemed askew. He'd disappeared
in the bathroom and was gone for more than twenty minutes. And when
he'd finally joined her in the marital bed, she sensed an agitation that was
new. She had been anxiously waiting for him, propped up against the
pillows in her trousseau nightie. It was mauve, layered with nylon frills.
She'd smiled bravely as he slid back into bed. Her glasses were on the
side table so she couldn't see the angst behind Reg's equally brave smile.

After a tentative hug and peck, they had turned off the light and
huddled under the blanket. Side by side, they gripped each other's
hand and waited. Her shaking and sudden tears distressed him. He
guessed the cause.

'We don't need to do anything,' he'd whispered into her hair. 'Lots of
bad things happened to me too when I was a kid. I'm not even sure if I can
do this. The awful memories keep coming back. I can't make them stop.'

That's when he'd told her.

What had happened moved him to another level of terror.
The searing pain, the hissed threats, the dazed staggering back to a
freezing bed. The shock of blood. Then the sleepless, foetal cowering

anticipating what became repeated nightly visitations. The pall of shame, which never leaves him, he'd said. It was there still: haunting his marriage bed. As he'd groped for words, flashbacks returned Reg to that dormitory of his childhood.

Sounds of snuffling, muffled sobbing and the creaking of iron beds fill his head. The kid next to him is Number 15 but his real name is David. He likes David. Sometimes they whisper to each before they fall asleep, huddled against the cold under a single grey blanket. The temptation to climb into the same bed for company and warmth is powerful but the thrashing that would await them at dawn prevents such an unwise decision. The doctor gives David a needle every night. Reg doesn't know why but David seems to be getting sicker and sicker. One night his bed is empty. Then Number 12 comes to sleep there instead.

The throb of chilblains on fingers and toes delays Reg's longed-for escape into another consciousness. That opportunity to move from panicky wakefulness to a space away from the everyday: a place with soothing, soft edges. The deep, deep sleep of childhood. Yet, even this peaceful repose is marred by the cold, wet sheets each morning indicating a deeper disquiet and triggering a new cycle of humiliation, beatings and deprivation.

But eventually even this special space is invaded as he is pulled from his bed to be taken to the toilets.

'Come on, sonny. You won't wet the bed if you go now,' slurs the voice in the dark.

2

His voice is barely a whisper. Janet doesn't question. She knows enough to fill the gaps and more words might become weapons. In the spacious bed, they are stones cast into a pond. Ripples surge into waves as she shivers in the dark until eventually her own terrors overwhelm. A sudden wave of nausea engulfs her as she stumbles into the bathroom. It is Mr White. He is still trapped inside her. His stinking breath and panting weight rushes back at her as she tries to breathe deeply and focus on the basin taps. The shuddering grows worse and she sobs as the vomit splashes up the sides of the porcelain bowl. The white tiles spin as she sits on the cold floor gulping air. It could be minutes or hours before she creeps back and slides under the blankets. Reg holds her tightly as her tears soak his shoulder and into the pillowslip.

Lurking memories dance around them, taunting and paralysing. But eventually they drift off to sleep. They greet a new day with faltering smiles, fortified by a gentle mantle of trust the night has delivered. It was to be many more weeks before they found the courage to consummate their union. It wasn't wild passion. Just a gentle searching for a way to give each other a sense of fleeting pleasure and enduring safety.

3

He had begun to count tiles. It filled the time now he spent so much of it seated on the new porcelain pedestal. He'd installed it himself and was proud of the professional finish he'd achieved. But Janet had noticed on a couple of occasions that he looked quite pale when he returned to his TV chair.

It was when Reg first mentioned the pain and bleeding that Janet formed her own opinion. It was because of the abuse, she concluded. However, after the preliminary medical examination, Janet's suspicions proved incorrect.

'So what did the doctor say?'

'Just some more tests. Nothing too serious, I reckon. It'll take care of itself,' he said.

So new tests were arranged. The picture became much murkier. A large shadow indicated a mass of delinquent cells. More tests. These were more invasive – and conclusive. Stage four.

Nonetheless, the oncologist was upbeat as he advised an aggressive approach. Cut, then poison. 'Don't worry, Mr Thomas. We see plenty of these and there's a chance we can beat it. Surgery first, then chemo to mop up.'

There was never any chance. It only took eight months.

Arrangements

'A parent's death was pivotal to children's futures. Often
the father could not cope with caring for the children after
his wife's death, whereas if a father died, the mother often
could not financially support her children… The attitudes of
the day also worked against some families staying together
as fathers were not seen as appropriate care givers…'
Forgotten Australians

The late afternoon sunlight ricochets off the regulation cream and green. Patches of empty space dance with dust motes, although how they have escaped the disinfectant is a miracle. The polished linoleum floor demands a shuffling gait similar to navigating icy pavements in different climes. There is no ice or snow here. The heat in Perth is peaking at this time of the year. It reached 105 degrees Fahrenheit yesterday and today doesn't feel much cooler.

As he settles on the chair by her bed, the sweat gradually pools under his thighs and thin buttocks.

How are you today, love?

The same question. There is no answer really. She's dying. That's how she is. And maybe she knows but keeps up the charade for his sake.

Not too bad. I had some jelly for tea tonight.

Her voice is quite bright. He's encouraged.

That's a good sign, isn't it? You'll come good with a bit more food in you.

Her arms are sticks and her collarbones are so sharp you could slice bread with them. Bob hasn't seen much of the rest of her for nearly two months now. She doesn't get out of bed any more. They bring the bedpan to her when she needs it.

And her colour is peculiar. A ghastly dark yellow. Like half brewed tea.

It's the jaundice, the ward nurse told him. *It always happens once the liver starts playing up.*

Playing up? What does that mean? The euphemisms befuddle him. Skirting around the reality that she looks worse and worse every day. Even he can see that. It's bloody obvious and no one has any decent answers.

Bob's head is pounding as he beats a well-worn track along the hospital corridors, through the heavy front door and down to the bus stop. A gecko on the wall of the bus shelter works at becoming as green as government transport paint. The patterned eyes seem to stare in every direction before a long tongue lubricates first one then the other. The translucent creature mesmerises. Bob wishes he could be so motionless and that his guts would stop their incessant churning. The tiny reptile lifts one webbed foot, freezes, then puts it down again. A fly settles on the peeling paint, oblivious to its camouflaged neighbour. A flash of pink tongue. Dinner. The bus arrives and Bob goes home for his.

Next day, he is at the hospital as usual. It's only slightly cooler and she looks the same.

How are the kids? Is Gwen managing all right?

He's noticed that she's finding it hard to concentrate properly now the morphine is muddling her mind. She says it mostly keeps the pain at bay but that the last hour of the four-hourly injections is always the worst.

They're okay, love. Nothing for you to worry yourself about.

Billy hasn't got that rash again, has he? The heat sets it off. Tell Gwen to use calamine lotion if it flares up.

You just stop worrying about that. Gwen's doing a good job. You need to save your energy and get well.

I know, Bob. I'll just close my eyes for a while.

Her once-pretty face looks like so many other dying faces. Time has been rubbed away and there is no clue to her age any more. The sunken eyes are circled with smudged pigment, the discoloured skin stretched tightly over the cheekbones, the grimacing mouth struggling to hold back pain. She exhales slowly and closes her eyes.

The doctors haven't told Bob much and he's noticed that they seem to be avoiding him lately. As he stares at the tiny form curled around the relentless pain, he barely recognises the bag of bones that was once his softly shaped Mary.

Bob's mind wanders as he lifts one buttock, then the other, trying to relieve the pins and needles. He stands up and stretches as he tries to piece together his unravelling life. He remembers that at first it was just the nausea, but eventually cramping pain left her doubled up over the sink.

I'm feeling off-colour, she'd admitted.

I reckon you look as yellow as a Chinaman, he'd joked. *You'd better get off to the doctor and find out what's up. Probably just need a tonic or something.*

The doctor was mystified but thought a short stay in hospital would give her a rest while some more tests were carried out. She had packed her best nighties, washed her chenille dressing gown, and Bob was confident that the doctors would fix the problem quickly. For the first week or so, the pain had settled with the medication and she had relished the luxury of time to shower and rub on Ponds cold cream each morning. She'd even shampooed her hair a couple of times and her dark waves looked quite lively. She was only thirty-four and had kept her shapely figure after the three children.

What have you done to yourself? You look as good as you did on our wedding day, he enthused during that first week at the hospital.

You can't fool me, Bob Marshall. I'm not looking that good but I had some time to do pin curls after I washed my hair. It's got some bounce back. And I'm not feeling too bad at all. A few more days and I'll be right as rain.

The kids are missing you. Be good to get you back home.

Have you remembered Friday is castor oil day? And don't let them go without a singlet. I know the weather's warming up but I don't want them to come down with a chill.

Don't worry, pet. We're managing all right. We just need to get you back on deck. I've brought you a few grapes. A couple of bunches are already ripe and I got them before those bloody parrots beat me.

Thanks, love. Put them on my side table and I'll have some in the morning with breakfast.

During this first week in hospital, Mary had enjoyed the attention and leisure time. The grapes Bob brought tasted tangy on her tongue, a relief from the bland, overcooked hospital food. The meals probably seemed worse because she'd noticed that the medication had created a metallic taste in her mouth. It was as though she'd been licking pennies. Despite this slightly nauseating side effect, she was feeling stronger and was keen for some kind of distraction. She hadn't seen the latest *Women's Weekly* but one of the nurses had told her that there was a lovely portrait of Princess Anne on the cover. Her own little Susie was the same age and with the same blonde curls as the Princess. Mary missed being in her own kitchen surrounded by her brood. She and Bob had made a good pair and created what most people would call a 'happy home'. Right from the beginning, Bob had taken an interest in the children and hadn't believed in belting them the way a lot of other fathers did. He was in no way a violent man and had never laid a hand on Mary or the children. She'd been lucky. So many other women she'd known seemed to cop a backhand for the slightest thing. Not that they mentioned it. Just covered the bruises with more powder. Even when Billy was a toddler and such a handful, Bob was always patient with him. His birth had been difficult and the doctors had told them that he might have slight brain damage.

Can't really be sure, they said. *Just have to wait and see whether he reaches his milestones at the right time.*

Which he hadn't. He was late with everything: rolling, sitting, standing, walking, talking, potty training. And at school he got more and more behind. He had to stay down last year and he still isn't doing too well. The girls, on the other hand, are as bright as buttons. Bob and Mary had been lucky there.

The weeks drag on and the antibiotics and various other medications prove useless. The vomiting returns more violently than before and her bloated abdomen is growing so tight and painful that she can hardly roll over. Her pee has become a horrible brown colour. Her hair is now lank without a skerrick of bounce. Her skin grows taut and more yellow. Her bones poke their way against her vanishing flesh. Looking down on her shrunken body, she doesn't resemble anyone she knows any more. Poor Bob barely recognises her. She is a stranger trapped in an alien bag of loose skin. A 'patient' whose parts can be prodded and poked without any need to address the head that is attached. Blurring and fading like an old photo, she is no longer a wife or mother. She is just an illness no one can name. What the team of experts had finally mumbled was that they couldn't do any more.

Bob looks for the gecko each evening as he waits for the bus. He usually finds it somewhere in the shelter, patiently waiting for midges and flies. Its colour changes according to the surface it sits on. Adaptation: a remarkable phenomenon. Always able to blend into the world you find yourself inhabiting. Bob wonders how much longer he can manage without Mary. He's not so good at adapting.

He is dazed by it all and just keeps plugging away at work, sitting by her bed each evening and falling exhausted into an empty bed where silent tears soak his pillow. The kids are wearing him down with their questions and his sister is beginning to grate on his nerves. As the weeks drag by, she begins to hint at the 'what if' scenarios.

Maybe you need to think about what will happen if Mary doesn't get better.

What she means by that he can't fathom. There is no other outcome as far as he is concerned. Mary will get better, come home and everything will be back to normal.

You're just going to have to face the facts. Gwen is raising her voice along with the stakes. *You'll have to make arrangements.*

For God's sake. Stop your harping, woman!

Arrangements. What the hell is she talking about?

The doctors will figure something out soon. No need to go jumping to any conclusions, Gwen. Could you just let me eat my tea in peace?

Putting your head in the sand, if you ask me, she mutters as she bangs down a plate of congealed stew.

His sister is not a hard woman, practical but not hard. She's very fond indeed of Mary and the kids.

I'm sure that you'd agree, Bob, a hotel is no place for children. So if the worst came to the worst, George and I would be in no position to take on the kiddies.

Bob acknowledges that it was very good of Gwen to come and stay. A Godsend if he's honest. Her husband George isn't a bad sort either. He'd encouraged her to help out when Bob's phone call had alerted them to Mary's illness.

Just for the time being, George had reminded Gwen.

So, the timeline, not formally drawn up, was nearing its end one way or another. What was 'too long' when it came to dying? Heart and brain and tissue sucked in oxygen for as long as possible and even clever doctors couldn't reliably predict when the whole system would collapse

The gecko gave him solace. He could drift in another world for a little while as he watched it day after day. He started to swipe at flies in an effort to feed the little fellow who was sometimes pale gold, sometimes green, and once a shade of pink as it clung to an abandoned and faded cerise cardigan. Its sticky splayed toes had balls of fluff attached. Like slippers, smiled Bob. He missed his bus once when he was stalking a fly around the back of the bus shelter.

The heatwave still hasn't broken. Day after day, the temperatures continue to soar and Bob's chair remains sticky. She opens her eyes only briefly now.

Hello, love. Have you had a good day? Her voice rasped as it worked at the air.

Not too bad. How's the pain today?

A little better this afternoon.

Just rest and I'll sit here for a while.

He wanted to tell her about the gecko but she couldn't stay alert long enough for him to share the wonder of its colours and patterned eyes. Instead of talking, he's got in the habit of bringing in the evening paper. Now he busies himself with the repetition of turning the pages. Sometimes he wishes he would never get to the end. Sometimes he starts from the beginning again just to maintain the soothing sound of paper moving through empty space. His eyes can see nothing on the pages. The curtain is drawn around her bed, which provides something more tangible to focus his mind. Searching for the tiny tears and broken threads in the faded green fabric, he counted fifty-five last night. This must be a new curtain. He can only find thirty-one.

There have been no arrangements made and no matter how hard he concentrates, he has no idea where to begin. At the bus stop that evening, he can't spot the gecko. He wanders a few feet away from the shelter, searching the footpath. On the concrete slabs behind the shelter he comes across its smashed form. He sobs uncontrollably over the tiny extinguished body.

After he's gone home for his tea, Mary rouses to an aluminium sky dazzling through the tall windows. Outside, the heat bounces off the domed ceiling of this parochial city wedged between a desert and an ocean. It seeps through masonry and glass into the stifling hospital ward. Matron has just completed her rounds and the patients are neatly arrayed with their counterpanes turned back four inches, corners tucked in and beds wrinkle free. As Mary sweats silently into the white starched sheets, she hazily imagines waves splashing over her. She's always loved the sea and she and Bob have taken the children to the beach each year during the summer. They catch the bus loaded up with towels and sandwiches and spend the day swimming and skylarking. By nightfall, the children collapse into bed exhausted, barely able to grin through faces that have turned into tight over-ripe tomatoes. Calamine is liberally applied and it takes another week before they can peel sheets of skin from each other's backs. A land of sun and sand and flies edged by an ocean of extraordinary power and beauty. A lucky place to be and a wonderful place to bring up children. Mary is certain of that. She longs for the cool of that ocean as she lies trapped in the clammy sheets.

A swim would be lovely, she mumbles to the empty chair.

Bob doesn't reply, so she drifts off without him. The waves embrace her. Become her. Liquid diamonds bounce off her skin. Her aquamarine swimsuit clings to rounded breasts and hips. She is cool. She is beautiful. She is as pearlescent as a nautilus shell. Wind and salt and spray fill her sails and she floats and floats and floats. Shells and sand whisper and spiral.

There is no pain.

That night, the duty nurse gently turns Mary's skinny body every four hours. The pressure marks are already showing on her bony buttocks, the scissor-sharp shoulder blades, the pathetic pointy elbows. Even her heels are beginning to inflame. The morphine dose is building up as she clings to life but eventually it will tip her over the edge.

Just tidying up the bed for you, she whispers as she rearranges the skeletal limbs. *I'll bring something more for the pain.*

It's the next dose that depresses Mary's breathing and slows her heartbeat to the point of no return. At dawn, she takes a final breath.

Mrs Marshall has gone, the night nurse reports at change-over. *I'll finish things for her before I go off duty. I'd like to do that. I grew very fond of her.*

She tests the water to make sure it's a comfortable temperature before she gently sponges the empty shell that had once been a pretty woman, a loving wife, a protective mother. And she opens the window to let Mary Marshall move freely away from earthly tribulations and the arrangements she will never have to make.

Witness

'Children were rarely given information about what was
happening, where they were going, where their parents or
siblings were and when they would next see them.'
Forgotten Australians

From the moment I arrived, visiting aunts and neighbours complimented my flawless complexion.

Just look at that beautiful face and those rosebud lips, they gushed.

I was the centre of attention and I admit that I enjoyed it. Despite the fact that my senses remain trapped beneath a china veneer, I can feel. Joy, excitement, pain – even grief. And my memory is quite remarkable. This may be of interest to those who believe the brain is the repository for all experiences, because my porcelain head is quite empty. Or you may be an animist and believe that despite my lack of a reasoning centre, I possess consciousness that allows me to move between the realms of the real and the imagined as I tell you about what happened all those years ago.

You may also believe that people are unable to remember events before the age of three or four years. Not constrained by notions of human development, it appears that I was created fully formed and time could not reshape me physically or mentally, although damage has been scribed onto my body. I have remained the same height and weight all my life and was assigned a consummate reservoir of knowledge. So I can recall the first time my legs were broken when I wasn't even a year old.

I spent three months at the hospital and Janet told me she missed me. The wide, anxious eyes peering from similarly frail and damaged bodies were my only company during those long weeks. No one visited.

No one comforted or cradled. It happened again sometime later. This time the protective arms became weapons as they flung me off the back veranda onto the concrete path. It was crazy paving that Dad had proudly sweated over the summer before. Crazy in a festive sort of way but concrete nonetheless. The damage was much worse, although a clod of weeds between the crazes partially protected my face. The hospital stay was even longer and my head still contains fragmented images of tangled legs and arms jumbled together. Missing features and bald scalps. A ghastly landscape of brokenness. And silence. Always the silence. It shimmered around me and made me uneasy.

I first met Janet in 1952 under the family Christmas tree. No fir tree this: instead, a banksia branch with golden candles poking through the tinsel. She loved me right away and named me Belinda. I was pleased with the name but immediately knew that it would take time for Janet to learn how to care. She dragged me by one leg to the festive table and my pretty yellow dress was covered in custard before the celebrations were over. By nightfall, I had been discarded and spent an uncomfortable night behind the couch. My inanimate state required that I waited patiently to be included in daily life. Janet's clumsiness and lack of attention led to the first accident. Her early apprenticeship in mothering proved inadequate and the unyielding linoleum of the bathroom floor did its worst. The dank surface could not absorb the force and my chubby white legs twisted at odd angles as the cold and damp seeped in. A tantrum was the cause of the second but after those early mishaps I never had to go back to the hospital. Janet became a dedicated and protective make-believe mother. She told me more of her secrets and we grew closer. She said that she still loved me even though my once-perfect china face now bore the chips and cracks of experience and my crooked legs never really mended properly. But this was a time when it wasn't unusual to see children who dragged a leg or hobbled in leg braces and built-up boots. Children who couldn't jump puddles any more.

Janet sometimes took me shopping and I can still see the mothers dressed in their second-best frocks and mended stockings adjusting their hats and smoothing their gloves as they sat side by side on the bus. Heaped on the grubby floor were string bags crammed with cabbages and potatoes and Vegemite and Dettol. More often than not, a select piece of liver oozed its bloody fluids through the butcher's paper and onto the bus floor. They exchanged gossip behind gloved hands.

You must have heard about that Gordon Swan – you know the Swans on the corner of White and Rose Street. Well, he's got the polio, you know. I heard it from Mrs Sampson and she always knows what's what. She says he's in the hospital in the iron lung thingy, touch and go for a while but looks like he'll live, be a cripple though, so Mrs Sampson says.

The mothers thanked their lucky stars that their Johnny or Beth hadn't caught the polio. They'd heard on the grapevine that there would be needles at the school soon that would stop the polio altogether. Well, what about the diphtheria? Mrs Binks wanted to know. Did it stop that too? None of the mothers were too sure about that but the doctors knew best and they would tell us when they were ready. It didn't pay to ask too many questions.

We always did things together, Janet and I. She used to tell me secrets that even Susie and Billy didn't know about. Like how she was going to be an air hostess when she grew up. She decided that carrying cups of tea on a tray high up in the sky required skills similar to a tightrope walker, so spent a great deal of time balancing her tea set on a plank of wood while walking along a skipping rope stretched across the backyard. She was also going to be a real mum one day.

She was practising this when she smacked me and said, *Belinda. I've told you a dozen times not to dirty your clean dress. Just eat your biscuit properly or you won't get another one.*

She was a good imaginary mother who knew what it took to mould a well-mannered and dutiful child.

We had a cubby between the passionfruit vine and the outside dunny and once we'd climbed inside, no one could see us. We had lots of afternoon teas with the rose tea set; sometimes with real tea leaves floating in cold water. I loved all our adventures. Some were pretty scary, like the time the crocodile that lived behind the shed chased her three times around the Hills hoist. Mum wasn't at all flustered when we ran inside to tell her.

It's just imaginitis. Crocodiles don't live behind sheds, she said. *Maybe it was a goanna.*

Janet and I were huffy about that. We both knew the difference between a crocodile and a goanna. We didn't bother telling Mum about Colin. He wasn't at all scary. His big furry face made us laugh when he hugged us in bed. Polar bears have got bad breath, though, and sometimes I wished that he would brush his teeth. If Janet was cross with me, she would only talk to Colin. I listened anyway.

There was another small accident when Janet poked me in the eye with the new pencil that Mum had bought her for school. Janet was five now and ready for Bub's class. It was excitement about starting school that caused her to wave the newly sharpened pencil while conducting an imaginary orchestra. She was practising 'God Save the Queen' ready for her first assembly. I just happened to be too close as the final bars were belted out. Janet was sorry that my eye looked so wonky but we all got used to it after a while, even though I did see two of everything most of the time.

Her first school day finally arrived and I waited to be collected.

With a new leather satchel on her back and virgin sandals squeaking, she plodded into the bedroom. *Dolls aren't allowed*, she said as she kissed me on the lips.

I was shocked. It had never occurred to me that Janet and I would spend whole days apart.

She usually left me sitting on a kitchen chair after breakfast; the kitchen was the hub of the household, so I didn't miss much. Now I had days to myself I became a witness to family events. Susie was still too little to go to school, so she was at home with me and Mum. Billy went to school but he had to stay down a year. The teacher said he couldn't be promoted to Standard Three because he didn't know his phonics or his two times table. Billy didn't care, because he said school was dumb anyway. He only liked being an Indian stalking the cowboys hidden on the spare block next door to our house. He crawled through the wild oats with chook feathers stuck in his hair. He never found the cowboys but it kept him busy most days after school. He should have been practising his times tables but he usually managed to escape that ordeal.

As soon as Mum put the chart on the table, he squirmed and moaned. *Arr, Mum, I've got a real bad tummy ache. I need to go to the dunny.*

It's a lavatory not a dunny, Billy, she'd cluck.

Maybe Mum knew that Billy's life would go on whether he knew his times tables or not.

I got quite lonely at home, because Susie didn't play with me. She was busy with her own tea set and her doll called Betsy. They mostly played under the kitchen table hidden behind a curtain of checked tablecloth. I could hear them whispering and laughing and felt very cross that I couldn't join in. I remained stranded on my hard kitchen chair until Janet got home. I daydreamed and made up stories to occupy myself when Mum and Susie went out shopping.

It was around this time I started to notice that Mum was bending over and taking deep breaths a lot. Her face would look crumpled and her eyes were scrunched shut.

Blessed cramps, she'd mutter. *I'm just going to have a little lie down,* she'd tell Susie.

I think Dad knew she wasn't quite right but he didn't say much when he got home because he was very tired from work and needed to read *The Daily News.*

Just give your father some peace, Mum used to say. *He needs a rest after a hard day's work.*

She never complained and we just had our tea and went to bed the same as usual. But from my kitchen chair I could see that Mum was leaning over the sink a lot more and her face was the same colour as the washing-up water. Her smiley watermelon mouth was upside down now.

Then one morning we got up and Mum wasn't even there. Our Aunty Gwen was making breakfast. Dad wasn't there either. The porridge was lumpy and we weren't allowed to have golden syrup on it.

A sprinkle of sugar is all you need. Golden syrup is a shocking waste. I'm not sure what your mother is thinking with such extravagances. She must know what a strain it is for your father to bring in enough for the whole family. Now I'm here, I can get things back on the straight and narrow.

She was so bossy.

What would she know, Janet whispered. *She's not even a real mum.*

When Dad finally came home, it was teatime. We had lots of questions but got no answers.

Where's Mum? Can we see her? When's she coming home? We don't like Aunty Gwen's mashed potato. There's lumps and black spots in it. And we couldn't have golden syrup on our porridge.

Stop worrying your father. He's got enough on his plate without that. Of course you can't see your mother. Children aren't allowed. Now brush your teeth and get to bed before I lose my wits.

Bossy as usual.

Dad was late home for tea every night now because he went to the hospital to see Mum after work. When he did get home, he would just say hello, nothing more. He never played the peekaboo game with us any more, just ate his dried-out chops and peas that had been sitting in the oven for ages. Didn't even read the newspaper and if you really looked you could see that his eyes just stared at something none of us could see.

Then one day Dad came home before tea. The front door slammed as his work boots travelled the unfamiliar surface of the carpet runner in the hallway. The shock of seeing the forbidden boots from our vantage point under the kitchen table brought our game to an abrupt halt while we waited for Aunty Gwen's fury. Instead she dropped the teapot. Tea leaves floated in brown rivers until miniature, black islands formed on the worn lino. We just stared as the floor took on its new landscape. Aunty Gwen's mouth seemed to have forgotten how to shape words. The kitchen froze into a world of silence. Thoughts and feelings were trapped in tiny jagged flakes filling the cramped room. Even the whining which had echoed around the backyard faded. Their squabbling suspended, Billy and Susie stood on the back doorstep, mouths open, staring at the kitchen tableau.

At last words came rushing back.

Shut that fly wire door before the flies get in. Get out from under that table while I clean this mess up. Early tea tonight and off to bed without any complaints. Janet, set the table. A boiled egg and toast soldiers is what we need.

Dad said nothing. His boots stayed under the kitchen table. The paint splashes made them look like confetti covering a giant's feet. He seemed to have forgotten how to move. He just sat like a splotchy statue in the gloom.

The sun was still creeping its way around the blinds when we got into bed but the bedroom door was shut tight by our aunty whose mouth looked like a dog's bottom. We grizzled about how early it was and started playing the I spy game. Billy had to sleep on the floor between our beds now that Aunty Gwen had the sleep-out.

Much later, we could hear an awful moaning noise but none of us knew what it was. Anyway, it stopped after a while so maybe it was just imaginitis as Mum would say.

We hardly ever saw our Uncle George, but here he was sitting at the kitchen table when we got up in the morning. Aunty Gwen plonked down grey porridge. The kitchen still seemed to be full of jagged pieces.

Even Uncle George's voice was cracked. *We're going for a drive in the Holden with your father.*

Aunty Gwen fussed about us all wearing our best clothes.

Where are we going? Is Mum coming? Can we have an ice cream?

No one answered.

Dad was already in front seat when we piled into Uncle George's car. His shoulders sagged inside the jacket of his best suit. We wondered in whispered voices whether we were going to the country. Mum and Dad had said that one day we would all go to the country for a holiday.

After what seemed forever, Uncle George stopped the car outside a kind of castle with a high wall and black gates. We all clattered out through the car door. Then we trailed behind Dad, through the gates and a huge wooden front door. Inside, standing on the shiniest floor I had ever seen, was a lady in white whose mouth pointed to our dad and formed the shape of a smile.

This is Mrs Goodman, Dad mumbled. *Say hello.*

Hello, my dears. What lovely children. Tell me your names.

Billy kicked Janet to make her go first.

My name's Janet and that's my brother Billy. He's eight and that's Susie. She's three.

We all kept staring at the shiny floor as Mrs Goodman smiled and smiled.

And how old are you, my dear?

I'm five already. And I'm in Bub's class.

Janet puffed out her chest.

And who is this? She pointed at me.

Belinda. She's got a wonky eye.

So she has, but what a pretty name. Now come along with me, all of you. This was our new home, she told us through her ghastly smile. *You can call me Matron*, she instructed.

The huge door banged and banged and banged, blocking the image of our dad shuffling away with his head bowed and arms hanging uselessly by his side.

Silence flooded into the enormous hallway with the shiny, shiny floor. Billy and Susie disappeared through a door. Janet and I waited and waited on a hard chair in another room until a skinny lady in a blue uniform brought us a glass of milk and an Anzac biscuit. I remember how Janet poked some biscuit into my still-perfect rosebud lips while she squeezed me tightly. At last Matron came back. Her splotchy face grimaced from behind the huge pillars of teeth. That's when the sound began to bounce off the smooth white walls as Janet screamed and kicked. Once again, my chubby legs were twisted under my body as I fell onto the glassy wooden planks. My wayward eyes captured two sets of leering teeth.

Come along, young lady. That's quite enough nonsense, Matron's not-so-friendly voice admonished through the shrill screams.

Rough hands gathered me up. A large key worried at a lock in a vast wooden door. The cupboard door closed, switching day to night. My legs remained at odd angles and my wonky eye stared at nothing. The dark smothered and silence engulfed me.

There were no more whispered secrets and afternoon teas with the rose tea set. A long time ago, I saw Janet. Only once. She came into the playroom and smiled at me but a big girl pushed her away and picked me up. A girl with spiteful hands.

Many decades have passed and I'm old now. My chipped and cracked pate has lost its beauty and even my rosebud lips have faded. My other eye is jammed shut and all the eyelashes have been picked out. Only a few strands of my yellow hair have survived. My legs have remained bent and my pretty voile outfit is quite shredded. No one plays with me now and I no longer inhabit the dark cupboard in the place where Janet used to live. The air around me is putrid and the seagulls screech incessantly overhead. I've been here for years waiting for the sun and rain to reduce me to smaller fragments. But china endures just like my memory. My hollow head remembers still.

Not Suitable for Children

'Nobody pondered the process of growing up, thought about
what went on in a child's mind, or attempted to understand it.'
Baby boomers: Growing up in Australia in the 1940s, 50s and 60s

The shelter shed

Sharon and Diane sit together in the lunch shed. The content of their
sandwiches informs the conversation.

'What have you got in yours today?'

'Jam.'

'Raspberry or apricot?'

'Raspberry. What's in yours?'

'Vegemite and cheese.'

'Lucky duck. That's my favourite.'

'Mine too.'

'Will you swap one for my jam?'

'Nup.'

'Denise Blower has Vegemite and beetroot in her sandwiches.'

'Erck. That's awful.'

'Yep. That's what I reckon too.'

Each munches in silence whilst gazing out towards the adjoining
bush reserve. Some screeching pink and grey galahs have distracted them.

'Do know that kid Billy in Miss Roberts's class?' asks Diane.

'You mean the spastic one?'

'He's not spastic. He's a slow learner, my mum said.'

'Well, I reckon he's spastic because he can't even do his two times
table.'

'That's not what spastic means. Spastic means you can't walk
properly. Billy's just a slow learner.'

'Well, I don't care what your mum says. How come she knows everything anyway?'

'She just does.'

'Well anyway, where is Billy? He hasn't been at school for ages.'

'I heard my mum tell my dad that he's gone away because his mum has passed on.

'What does "passed on" mean?'

'I dunno. Dead or something.'

Sharon doesn't know quite what to do with this startling information. 'I don't care. He's just a stupid boy. And I hate boys,' she says as she stalks off to play with someone else.

Diane is just too big for her boots sometimes.

Not for children's ears

Sharon's mother has one of her heads coming on. She's comforted by the captioned image on the packet of Bex powders. The reassuring smile of the white-veiled nurse who asks, 'Stressful day? What you need is a cup of tea, a Bex and a good lie down.'

Sharon's mum knows that's precisely what she needs. Today it's been one thing after another. Firstly the chooks getting out of the yard and up the lane. It took most of the morning to get them all back in and tie up the broken pickets. She'll have to remind Tom about fixing the fence. Then the new lemon cake recipe had proved disastrous and she'd wasted four eggs and half a pound of butter. Finally, her most modern appliance had clogged up when something she couldn't identify had got sucked up the hose. The outdated but more reliable carpet sweeper was summoned back into action. She certainly hoped that Tom could sort out the problem. The vacuum cleaner wasn't even a year old.

She is steeling herself for the arrival of her rowdy and rather unladylike daughter. Who doesn't disappoint as she crashes through the fly wire door spattering news like vomit into the pristine kitchen.

'Diane said that Billy's mum passed on and that he's gone to live somewhere else and that he won't come back to our school any more.'

Her mother exhales slowly as she places a plate of milk arrowroot biscuits and a glass of milk on the table.

Sharon takes advantage of her mother's momentary silence. 'Anyway, why would he do that when he's already got a house to live in? He's got a little sister. She's in Bubs with Miss Parkes. I don't like Miss Parkes. She's really strict. She smacks the Bubs kids on the legs with a ruler.'

The kettle whistles and her mother warms then fills the teapot, turning it three times in each direction before gently swaddling it in the tea cosy. A brown tea cosy with yellow daisies embroidered around the edge. An unexpected gift from her sister last Christmas. They had previously only exchanged cards. She must remember to send her something this coming festive season.

'Diane said that Miss Roberts sends Billy to the headmaster's office all the time because he can't do spelling and sums. Her desk is near the door so she can see him going past our class. Mr King always gives the boys the cane when they go to his office. Then they have to sit on the veranda and eat their play lunch by themselves. Billy is always on the veranda poking his tongue out. Diane reckons he's a slow learner.'

Her mother's head pounds despite the Bex. News of tragedy so close at hand is always very upsetting. Although, as Sharon's mother realises, the source of this information is not entirely reliable. She must remember to ring Vera and ask her what she knows about it.

'For Heaven's sake, Sharon. My head is splitting. Will you just give me a moment's peace?'

Sharon chomps through her milk arrowroots. Her mouth is too full to relay any more important news but her mother has some sound advice before she goes to have a lie down.

'Let me remind you, Sharon, there are some things that are not for children's ears. Whether Billy comes back to school or not is of no concern to you. And children certainly shouldn't be discussing such morbid things as death. Now go and play outside until teatime and keep out of your father's way when he gets home. I'm sure he won't want to listen to your incessant clatter.'

Sharon is tempted ask what 'morbid' means and whether passed on really means dead. She's seen a dead budgie and it didn't 'pass' anywhere. It stayed where it was and looked like it was asleep. However, Sharon is cognisant of the fact that adults know what is best for children and that asking questions is usually pointless.

'And another thing, Sharon. I was disappointed to notice that you've broken one of your father's tomato stakes. I don't think he'll be very pleased to see that when he does the watering. Let's hope he has had a good day.'

Sharon had forgotten the tomato stake but now, reminded, she feels jittery. Her father has a terrible temper.

Scatters and overhand

It's knuckle-bone season. Sharon has finally got a full set of five.

'We had soup last night and Mum gave me the knuckle-bone. Do you wanna play?'

'Yep. Scatters or overhand?'

'Overhand. But don't forget no sweeping. That's the rules.'

Sharon and Diane rush through the routine of deciding who goes first.

Eeny, meeny, miney, mo,
Catch a nigger by the toe.
If he hollers let him go,
Eeny, meeny, miney, mo.

It's Sharon. They settle cross-legged on the wooden veranda. It's the best spot. Shady but near the rails so they can keep an eye on the playground. They can see Denise sitting in a circle on the asphalt with four other girls. She isn't playing knuckle-bones today. She is still glowing from being the first kid at school to have a plastic set. Her celebrity has allowed her entrée to the favourite girls' gang. The game is Chinese Whispers and Denise's face is serene as she bends her head to receive a whisper.

'Did you see Denise's knuckle-bones? They're coloured and not even made of bones.'

'She always thinks she's so smart. Where did she get them?'

'At the Royal Show, she reckons.'

'Mum said that we can't go to the Royal Show. She says it's just a waste of money.'

'Yeah, my mum said that.'

'Denise got three show bags. They must be rich or something.'

Their game lacks its usual competitive edge. They are both preoccupied with dreams about show bags and real plastic knuckle-bones. The bell goes and they shove their way into the class line. Sitting up straight with arms folded, they wait for Miss Asher to hand out their Social Studies books.

'Open at the next clean double page. No, Geoffrey. That is not a double page. Will you please listen to what I am saying.'

Miss Asher has a smudge of red chalk dust on the back of her dress, which sets off a wave of sniggering around the room.

'Today we are copying the Union Jack onto the blank page and writing the words on the lined page. Remember the colouring must be your neatest. Do you understand, Geoffrey?'

Geoffrey is nearly the dumbest kid in the class. Sharon saw his half-yearly report when he dropped it on his way to the bike rack. She had a quick look before she gave it back. Miss Asher's comment was *Geoffrey is a nuisance in class and needs to pay more attention. Improvement is required in all subjects.*

His class position was forty-third. Sharon was twelfth. Denise, of course, was first.

Sharon opens her pencil tin as Miss Asher points to the blackboard, where her chalked illustration sets an exemplary standard. Rearranging the coloured pencils, Sharon can't remember whether violet comes before indigo.

'Stop fiddling with those pencils, Sharon. You only need blue and red.' Miss Asher is now seated at her desk but can see as well as any bird of prey.

Sharon wishes the flags they drew had purple on them.

The public address system crackles and Mr King clears his voice.

Attention, teachers, boys and girls. Congratulations to Miss Parkes's class for having the tidiest bags today. I am very sorry to report that two boys were caught throwing stones at recess time. I must stress that this type of behaviour is not acceptable. A reminder to all classes that tomorrow is folk dancing practice on the assembly area. We only have four more weeks before the end-of-year concert, so I expect everyone to be doing their very best and anyone seen disrupting practice will be sent to my office immediately. Thank you for your attention. Teachers, you may proceed with your lessons.

At least it won't be Billy who mucks up the lines at folk dancing, thinks Sharon. Whether it's her concern or not, she has noticed that he still isn't at school.

Have you heard?

Sharon's mum has five minutes to herself at last and rings Vera.

It's Carol here, Vera. How are you, my dear? Yes. I'm sorry I missed the meeting. I had one of my heads. No. The doctor doesn't seem to be much help. Maybe I just need a tonic. What about you? And how are the children? That is good news. Sharon's well, thank you. She did tell me something rather upsetting, though, and I was wondering if you've heard anything about the Marshalls who live in Tate Street? At number 44. We don't really know them very well. I think he's a painter or something like that. Two of the children go to the primary school. Yes. That's right. Well, I'd heard that she was quite ill in hospital but there's a whisper that she might have passed on. Yes. It's dreadful news. Yes. Three kiddies. The oldest is a spastic boy. The others are girls. Tragic. I agree with you, Vera. A man couldn't manage three children on his own. Of course. You could never be sure that it would be a suitable environment for youngsters. Just a minute. I can hear Tom coming in from work. I must get his tea on the table, so I'll hang up now, dear. Do let me know if you hear any news about Mrs Marshall. Bye bye for now.

Steak and kidney pie

Sharon's mum has taken the opportunity to pop down to the butcher shop before the heat builds up. She has just remembered that the Fortes are neighbours of the Marshalls and may have some news about Mrs Marshall's situation. She finds it increasingly disturbing that someone as young as Mrs Marshall may have died. It makes her think about her own mortality and she wonders about her headaches. Even three powders a day don't seem to be making a difference.

She puts on her bright face as she enters the butcher shop. 'What warm weather we're having, Mr Forte. Just a half a pound of that skirt steak today, thank you. Perhaps a few kidneys too, if you have any. I'll make a steak and kidney pie. It's always a favourite.'

Mr Forte – Jim to those who know him better – weighs the steak and a few kidneys before he parcels it all up in a neatly cut square of white paper. Unlike many butchers, he is a man of few words, but this does not deter Sharon's mum, who is quite skilled at keeping a conversation moving.

'By the way, I was wondering if you've seen Mrs Marshall about recently? I heard on the grapevine that there's some sort of problem in the family. And of course, I thought that if anyone would know it would be you and Betty, being neighbours of the Marshalls.'

'You'll have to ask Betty,' he says.

He has no opinion to offer. His wife specialises in opinions.

'A good idea. I'll drop in and see her. I need to return her cake plate from our school mothers' committee meeting. Thank you, Mr Forte. Have a pleasant day.'

Neighbourly concern

'Come in, Carol. How lovely to see you. I'd almost forgotten about that plate. Let me put the kettle on. I've just finished the polishing and I'm ready for a sit down.' Betty hurriedly tidies her hair and removes her housecoat.

Carol follows her down the passage into the kitchen. Drifting at the window are bright café curtains, which are the latest thing. On the counter is a very smart red Mix-master.

'What gay colours, Betty. And Laminex! It must be so easy to wipe down.'

Betty is proud of her modern kitchen. She and Jim like to keep up with the times without appearing ostentatious. She allows just a flicker of a smile to register in response to Carol's enthusiastic appraisal. 'That is kind of you to say, Carol. I chose the décor myself, actually. I had the option of coral pink but the two-tone red marble was the latest, so I took the plunge.' Betty strokes the smooth surface dreamily.

'I won't stay long, Betty. But there was something that I was concerned about. Your neighbours the Marshalls. I've heard there were some problems there. Some suggestion of a bereavement in the household.'

'I did hear a whisper, but nothing official. To be honest, I've never seen much of Mrs Marshall, just occasionally at the letter box, and he always goes off very early to work. The three kiddies play out in the backyard mostly. They're quite rowdy sometimes, especially the spastic boy.'

Betty serves the tea with a slice of lemon cake before she continues. 'I did know that she's been in hospital, because the aunt has been staying there for weeks. She said hello over the back fence and told me that she was looking after the children while her sister-in-law was in the hospital.'

The teapot is drained before Betty adds, 'I have to admit that since Sunday I haven't heard the children at all.'

Carol finishes her second cup. 'It must be serious to be in hospital so long. More than women's troubles, you would think, wouldn't you?' she says.

'Oh, definitely something serious. I did wonder if it might be a growth. I've heard that these things can take off very quickly. Depends where they are of course, but Gloria told me about a woman she knew who was gone in a few weeks. It was the liver, I believe.'

Carol's face clouds as her own unexplained headaches swim into her mind. She collects herself and smooths her frock. 'Oh, I do hope it's not that. What an awful thought. I'll keep a look out in the newspaper. If something terrible has happened, I would think that the aunt would put in a notice. Thank you for the tea, Betty. Lovely lemon cake. I must get the recipe some time.'

Betty is still dredging her mind for clues. 'Now that I think about it, there has been quite a lot of unusual coming and going the past day or so. The uncle has been there. I know because he's got a green Holden that I've seen out the front. A very popular car, according to Jim.'

Sewing, manual and monkey bars

'I hate school.'

Sharon kicks the dirt on the school track that she and Diane are trudging along. The days go on and on and the summer holidays seem forever away.

'Yeah. So do I,' says Diane.

Billy hasn't come back, but everything else is the same at school. Boring old marching in pairs, saying tables, colouring in stupid maps of England and the Empire.

'And I really hate spelling and dictation,' spits Sharon, who is sick of writing out her spelling mistakes twenty times each.

In fact, the main thing Sharon looks forward to is the compulsory quarter-pint of milk at recess time. Even if the bottles have been sitting in a crate in the sun for hours. She doesn't care about the slightly curdled texture or the collapsing paper straws.

'What have we got today?' she asks, hoping for a miracle.

She imagines that Denise could casually say, 'Oh, today is playing outside until lunchtime. Then it's sport all afternoon.' Sharon loves sport. She's a really fast runner.

However, today is actually Wednesday, so it's scripture before lunch and sewing and manual in the afternoon. She hates scripture too, because she's a Methodist and gets sent to the lunch shed with all the Other Denominations. They have to do silent reading under a corrugated roof which broils and crackles in the heat.

As she remembers the real order of the day, she groans. 'I wish I was Church of England or a Catholic like you, Diane. It's not fair. You get to have real ministers and proper colouring-in books with holy pictures.'

She'd seen Diane's book full of palm trees and stone archways. It was beautiful – always shaded in pastel colours. Although Diane did admit that she'd got into trouble early in the year. She had coloured a toga bright pink and added green polka dots.

'And you get to wear a bride's dress when you do that special church thing. I wish I could do that.' Sharon's voice is beginning to whine like a blocked vacuum cleaner. 'Anyway, I might be a nun when I grow up,' she declares.

She's seen a few nuns and is in awe of the black and white habit with the interesting knick-knacks hanging around the waist.

The morning drags into the afternoon, which stretches into eternity. The room is stifling and the blowflies that have bashed themselves to the edge of life are lined up on the window ledge. The listless silence in the classroom is interrupted by volleys of death buzzes.

Sharon sighs loudly as she tries to kick Geoffrey's legs under the desk in front of her. She can't quite reach, so settles for an insult. 'Yuk. I can see nits in your hair, Geoffrey Tyler,' she whispers as she leans forward.

Geoffrey ignores her. He has lost interest in the day and has forgone his favourite occupation of pulling the wings off the stranded flies. He picks his nose and examines the snot in a desultory sort of way.

There has been no sea breeze this afternoon. Miss Asher's vase of peonies has collapsed into a sad starfish. It's a pity, because they came fresh from Denise's mum's garden this morning. Denise is Miss Asher's pet.

'Sharon, stop talking and get on with your silent reading.'

Miss Asher's voice is like sandpaper. It scratches and grates. On and on. 'Just pay attention, everyone. Today at sewing and manual time, all the girls are to go into Miss Roberts's class. Boys, you will go to Mr Hollings as usual. I will be assisting the visiting nurse. Girls, collect your baskets and remember, no talking during sewing time. Good afternoon, everyone.' Her voice is snappy.

'Good afternoon, Miss Asher.' A weary sing-song response.

The afternoon recess bell clangs and a crush of sweaty bodies smelling of orange peel and piddle race to be first in the line. Sharon and Diane are first out the door. They usually are. They have learnt to use their elbows.

'Quick, Sharon! Bags the monkey bars before that Susan does. I can do an over-the-moon with no hands.'

'That's dumb, Diane. You can't do an over-the-moon with no hands. You're just doing an apple-turnover. Anyone can do those.'

'Just shut up, Sharon. You think you're so smart. I don't even want to be your friend any more.'

'I don't care. You're just a skite.'

Recess time is short. It is supposed to be a lavatory break only. Only one trick has been performed on the monkey bars before the bell goes. The ex-friends do not agree on what it is called.

No talking

'Come in, girls. You'll have to share a desk today. Are you all still working on the pot-holders? If you're ready, come and get your piece of material for the backing. Line up at my desk and no talking in the line.'

There's a scramble and the line already snakes as far as the door.

'What on earth is this mess, Jackie? You'll have to go and unpick it. Next person.'

Sharon and Diane are seated at the same desk despite being sworn enemies.

Miss Roberts knows who needs to sit where. 'Sharon, there is no need for that chatter. What are you talking about anyway?'

'Nothing, Miss.'

'Well, it can't be nothing if it takes so many words to say it. Come out the front and tell us all what is so important that you have to disturb everyone while they are working. Well, young lady? What was it that you're so keen on gossiping about?'

Sharon gets up from her seat. 'I was just asking Diane about Billy Marshall, Miss. She says that he isn't coming back to school because his mum died.'

The small black buttons that are Miss Roberts's eyes bore into Sharon, who stares at her grubby toes poking out of the battered sandals.

Miss Roberts's voice is as unbending as steel. 'I'm sure that is none of your business, Sharon. I don't expect to hear any more about it. Go and sit at the back of the room with your sewing for the rest of the afternoon. We don't need any more gossiping about things that have nothing to do with us.'

Mothers know best

'How was school today, love?' Her mother is quite bright.

'Okay I s'pose. But I hate Miss Roberts. We had to go to her room for sewing today and she made me sit up the back by myself for nothing.'

Sharon's mum reminds herself that the maidenhair ferns will need attention after such a hot spell. 'Sharon, I've told you before we should never use the word "hate". I'm sure Miss Roberts must have had her reasons. I'm going to water the ferns on the side veranda, so stay outside until your father gets home. And wipe your feet properly before you come back in. The chooks are out for a pick.'

On an even brighter note she adds, 'Shepherd's pie tonight for tea. Your favourite.'

It's not really Sharon's favourite but her mother always knows best.

'Has that Billy Marshall been back at school yet?'

'Dunno.'

The fly wire door bangs shut. Chooks flap like coloured bits of rag.

Official news

MARSHALL (Mary Susan) of 44 Tate Street, Leederville. Passed away on 20 November, 1954, at Royal Perth Hospital. Beloved wife of Robert James, loved mother of William, Janet and Susan. Fond sister and sister-in-law of Mr and Mrs G.M. Smith of Guildford.

R.I.P.

For the Good of the Kiddies

'Access visits by parents…were often denied due to apparently subjective decisions of departmental officers and as a form of punishment for a child's behaviour or parents falling behind in fee payments. Family visits to children were regarded as a privilege to be withdrawn rather than a right…little effort was made to encourage or facilitate the maintenance of connection with parents or family.'
Forgotten Australians

Bob stumbles from room to room looking for something. Anything to focus his mind and fill the gaping hole that gnaws at his guts. But as he crosses each lintel into a space once occupied by those he loved, he is driven back by a force mocking his anguish.

There's no one here, the one-eyed teddy bear shouts. *She's gone, she's gone, she's gone*, the clothes in the wardrobe hiss.

He slams the doors on the jeering voices and eventually finds a pocket of silence in the hallway where he drags some bedding and falls into a deep sleep. But the voices slide under the closed doors and invade his dreams with terrifying sounds and images. Howling mouths shriek and sob. He thrashes and cries and prays to a God he now doubts but can't entirely reject.

His dreaming terrors finally retreat. His waking nightmares return. He creeps into the kitchen to make a cup of tea and eat Gwen's dried-out ham sandwiches.

Gwen and George made all the arrangements. And paid for the funeral.

'It's the least we can do,' George had said.

These were the only few words his brother-in-law had muttered, but his sister had many more to offer.

'A man can't raise children on his own, Bob. It's for the best and I'm sure the home will provide all the right things that kiddies need. That's why all those good souls take in children from unfortunate situations. You can visit, and you never know, your circumstances might change one day.'

Bob had been unable to make sense of Gwen's incessant stream of noise. The words fluttered around him like falling leaves and lay at his feet in rotting piles. He could only scuff at them with his boots pushing them away. And away. Words and words and words. They had battered him and left him with nothing to grasp. They made him feel as weightless as the film of dust that had settled on his best black shoes as he'd stood by Mary's grave.

A dishevelled stick man against a sky of relentless blue.

Head bowed, hat in hand, his only suit shabby and flapping like a tired tablecloth in the hot wind. Mute and motionless, he'd stood and stood with the sun beating down.

He had become the space a man once filled. Nothing more than the sum of essential elements: oxygen, carbon, hydrogen, nitrogen, calcium and phosphorus. Still a living organism consisting mainly of water, and like water he had become if not transparent, at least translucent. Anyone would have seen straight through him if they met him on his way to the bus stop. A shade, a spectre, a ghost.

It was over. His beloved Mary was a collection of decomposing cells beginning their transformation into dust. And his three beautiful children were in good hands. According to all those around him.

The kitchen is grey. His tears have washed away any colour. His tea tastes grey and the sandwiches are filled with something grey. Perhaps the world will always be grey, he thinks. Patches of brightness have been erased from his world.

It was Gwen who had organised the telegram to Mary's parents announcing her death. Their return telegram consisted of seven words. *Heartbroken. Not able to be with you.*

Six weeks on a ship to see their daughter's gravestone would have been too much to bear. Even if they had the money.

At last, his well-meaning, noisy sister had left. The house continued to roar its emptiness.

Weeks slipped by in a blurry haze. There seemed no edges to his day and his nights remained fractured by unwelcome horrors. At work, Bob was a machine. He was a painter by trade and worked at the local racecourse. There wasn't much focus required to paint white rails over and over again. His work hadn't always been rails. There were plenty of buildings and structures on the grounds that needed maintenance but his boss kept sending him out to the rails. Waiting to see some sign of life returning to the shape called Bob.

The first visiting day at the home was still a few weeks off. No visits were allowed for the first six weeks. He'd been told by the matron that this was normal. It was to assist with the transition process.

'They need to become familiar with the routines of their new home. Too much outside interference is often quite disruptive,' she'd explained.

Bob's fogginess slowly receded. His edges took on more definition. His clogged mind was at last creating spaces filling with thoughts of the children. His beloved children. He missed their high-pitched voices and laughter. He missed tripping over the tricycle as he came through the gate each evening. He missed their warm, soap-smelling essence each evening as they scrambled onto his lap for a bedtime hug. The ache was bottomless. His love, crushing. He wondered how he could even express his love across such a gulf of distance and time. How to reassure them about how precious they were. About how hard he was working so that one day they could come home. The only possible contact seemed to be via letters, even though they were too young to read properly. If he enclosed some gifts with a letter, that might help cheer them up. He presumed that the home would have had a Christmas party with gifts from Santa. Even Billy still believed in a jolly, fat man coming down the chimney. But a present from their dad would be special and maybe would help reassure them of his abiding love.

Bob struggled with the brown paper and string. It was usually Mary who had organised and wrapped up presents. At last, the corners stayed folded and he tied the string in a double knot.

For Billy, there was a cap gun and a roll of caps. Billy's chook-feathered noggin sticking up over the wild oats flashed back into Bob's mind and made the corners of his mouth slant towards a smile. Billy never caught the cowboys. He'll have to change sides now, Bob realised. The bow and arrow set was beyond his budget.

For Janet, there was a beautiful tin of Lakeland coloured pencils. She loved colouring in and was getting really good at staying inside the lines. Bob felt certain that the home would have paper for drawing and pictures for colouring-in.

And for Susie there was the little knitted golliwog that Mary had bought at the school fete. It had been hidden at the back of Bob's sock drawer intended as a birthday present for Susie when she turned four. That was still some time off but it wouldn't hurt for her to have it early, he thought.

He posted the parcel off to the home.

5 January 1955

Dear Matron

I am sending presents for Billy and Janet and Susie. I know that it is too late for Xmas but I lost track of the days. I'm sorry about that but I wasn't myself for quite a while. Inside the parcel there is a letter for them all. Could you let Billy read it to his sisters, please. He might need some help because he's a bit backward. I hope that they are all behaving properly. Please let them know that I am looking forward to my first visit, which isn't very far away.

Yours sincerely

Robert Marshall

At the end of the six-week waiting period, Bob goes down to the phone box and telephones the home to organise his visit. The visiting hours are between two p.m. and four p.m. on the first Sunday of the month, he is informed. Bob has missed the January visit and would have to wait until February. Another three weeks away.

These slightly crackly words bounce off the glass of the telephone box. 'Are you still there, Mr Marshall?'

The constriction around his throat almost blocks the air completely. Words come at last. Shaky and faint. 'But I've waited the six weeks. Surely this is a special situation and I can see them before then?'

The answer is no. There are no special situations. Rules are to be followed in order to maintain standards. Matron would send a letter reporting on the children's progress.

Bob replaces the earpiece. His eyes remain fixed on the black Bakelite communication device. An urge to smash it out of existence engorges him.

A ruddy-faced woman taps on the glass, at first discreetly and then impatiently.

He stumbles home.

Weeks passed. There was no letter. He stopped hurrying to the letter box as soon as he arrived home from work. The resident redback spider in the little house on a post sometimes shared the space with a few bills, but nothing else. At times, his mind started spinning again and in the kaleidoscopic jumble of sounds and images, Matron's stern words returned.

'As I've stated, our policy is that family wait the stipulated time before their first visit. It is not fair on the kiddies to upset them unduly. I'm sure you would agree with this, Mr Marshall.' She was as imposing and as hard as the stone walls surrounding the home.

'We don't like to encourage unnecessary contact with family members. The children need to understand that this is their new home. Policies must be followed by all staff and we can't make exceptions.

That's what children need. Routine and discipline. We all know that it's for their own good, don't we, Mr Marshall.'

For their own good? It didn't make any sense to him then and it still doesn't. How can such a shocking change to their whole world not be terrifying for young children? No one seemed to consider this likelihood. No, he didn't agree with Matron.

But he'd slunk away without a word. At the time, he could find none to express the flooding of grief, of confusion, of futility, of despair. Words had become useless as they danced around in his brain and could find no way to make their way out.

As he recalls this initial meeting with Matron, his sense of helplessness returns. Does he have no say in what happens to his children? This isn't how he'd expected to be treated. It's as if he is some sort of undesirable drifter rather than a dedicated father.

Bob clung to his routines: rising at dawn, catching the bus to and from work, feeding the chooks, watering the yard and getting himself dinner. Mostly boiled eggs and potatoes followed by bread and jam with his cup of tea. He didn't know much about cooking and he didn't much care what he ate. He had Saturday afternoon and Sunday off and that's when he really struggled with the emptiness. He mowed the bit of grass and washed his work clothes in the trough. He'd give the kitchen floor and veranda a sweep. He knew that he should wash the sheets on his bed and the greying bath towel he used each day but he couldn't summon up the energy required to chop kindling and light the copper. He mostly filled the empty hours sitting in a cane chair on the back veranda smoking his Capstans and staring at the wooden palings of the back fence. Then he went to bed.

He continually fought to suppress his longing to see the children. Of course, he didn't want to upset them more than necessary. But, more than two months had passed and he still hadn't been able to visit them. The home was nearly twenty miles away and the logistics of how to get there by public transport on a Sunday had Bob baffled. There was no train or bus that took him close to the property, but a chap from work who had a car had offered to drive him up to there. He was so grateful. He'd always thought Fred was a snob. He seemed to big-note himself and talked a lot about getting new things for his house. But Fred didn't have any kids and since his promotion to supervisor he could afford more than Bob, that was for sure. Bob was paying the home every month and with three children, it mounted up. Fred wasn't a bad sort after all.

They were having smoko in the lunch shed the week before Bob's Sunday visit was due. Fred had changed his mind – or his wife had changed it for him.

'The wife says it's a waste of a Sunday afternoon to drive all that way. I feel sorry about your kids but I just can't help you out after all. Sorry, mate.'

Bob was wordless.

But at last the all-important Sunday arrived and with a surge of determination, Bob set off early on a trip consisting of a number of bus journeys that eventually got him what he estimated was four or five miles away from the home. His rather muddled directions took him on a meandering route through bush tracks. It took him two hours to walk the final distance but he arrived by one forty-five p.m. He entered through those same massive doors that had swung so resoundingly closed on him that terrible day in November. There was a sign pointing to a waiting room. He sat on the hard chair and waited. A wall clock ticked its way loudly to two o'clock. He stood up, retrieved the bag of sticky sweets from his pocket and took a deep breath.

Matron met him in the hallway. 'Good afternoon, Mr Marshall. I understand that you are here to see the children but it appears that your payments have fallen into arrears. I'm sorry to inform you that until that is rectified, we are unable to arrange a visit.'

Bob had forgotten the monthly postal order.

'It's a matter of the rules, Mr Marshall. I am sorry you've travelled to no avail. But, I'm sure everything will be in place for next month's visit. Good day, Mr Marshall.'

15 February 1955

Dear Matron,

I am sorry to bother you when I know how busy you must be but I was wondering how the children were managing. Did they like the presents I sent? Did Billy manage to read the letter okay? Maybe Janet helped him. She is quite a good little reader already even though she is only five. I have made up the late payment as we arranged. Please reassure the children that I will visit next month on the first Sunday. And please give all the children my love.

Yours sincerely,
Robert Marshall

Work, home, dinner, bed. And he still hadn't had a visit. He finally lit the copper and boiled the sheets and towels. By the time he'd rinsed them, put them through the wringer twice and hung them out to dry, he felt buggered. A woman's work wasn't so easy and memories of his pretty Mary, who was always cheerful even on washing day, swamped his empty, empty soul. Tears flooded his washed out eyes and ran in torrents down his scraggy face. He sat and sat and sat in the cane chair, staring at the palings, which unlike every other aspect of his life, never changed.

22 February 1955

Dear Matron,

Even though I haven't heard from you, I wonder whether it would be possible for you to send one or two of the children's drawings? It would give me great pleasure to have something from them and I know that they are not really old enough to send a letter. Well, Billy might be but as I explained before he is behind with his reading and writing. I hope the payments are arriving on time. Please remind them that I will be there next visiting day.

Yours sincerely,
Robert Marshall

The little gabled house on a post remained empty.

'Had a chance to visit your kiddies yet?' asks Fred from work.

'Not yet, Fred.'

He'd briefly mentioned his abortive attempt, but couldn't go into the details. He knew that he'd break down if he tried. 'I was expecting a letter from Matron but I haven't heard a word. It just seems so hard to keep in touch with the poor little beggars. How would they be feeling about their dad not seeing them? They'd think I didn't even care.'

'Let me talk to the wife again,' says Fred.

At smoko a few days later, Fred makes another offer. 'The wife said she'd like to help out. But just the once, she said. We can't be a taxi service, she said.'

Bob is tearful and thanks his lucky stars for a good bloke like Fred. And his missus.

He makes sure his suit is aired and brushed. He struggles with the iron but eventually manages to smooth the front of his only white shirt. He picks up his hat and the little bag of boiled sweets. He senses the nearness of something to hold onto.

The car ride is quiet. Fred's missus isn't a talker, which suits him. They drop him at the gate.

'We'll go off for a little drive and meet you back here at four o'clock,' says Fred.

'Much obliged,' says Bob. 'See you then.'

He sits on the wooden bench outside Matron's office. He's ten minutes early and he's feeling nervous.

'Do come in, Mr Marshall. I need to talk to you before you go to the visitor's room.'

Matron's voice is grave and her face is furrowed. The brusque manner that he has previously experienced seems tempered as she offers the chair.

'Please, sit down. I am most dreadfully sorry to have to break this news to you, Mr Marshall. It's explained in the letter here. I was to post it off in the morning. It's about your daughter Susan. She has been very unwell recently. Diphtheria. Tragically, we have been unable to save her despite the doctor's best efforts. It was just two days ago, I'm afraid.'

Bob's gaze is fastened to the desk lamp. It has a brass stand and green shade. If he just keeps staring, the world will vanish. There will only be a green desk lamp and nothing else. Forever. He won't need to take any more breaths, because the world won't exist. There will be no more sounds, no more words. Words and words and words. Pouring out of the ghastly gash in Matron's face and smashing around him. And the air is too solid to go in and out of his lungs any more. And his arms thrash like storm swept branches as he clutches at the edge of Matron's desk.

After minutes or maybe years, more words reach his ears.

'I am most terribly sorry, Mr Marshall. You have my deepest sympathy. I realise that it must be a dreadful shock but you must be reassured we did everything possible. Little ones can go so suddenly with these illnesses. I will forward on any documents the doctor might have left. We have taken care of everything for you already. There is nothing you need to do.'

There is no air to breathe. No words to shape the pain that smothers him.

'Try to hold yourself together, Mr Marshall. Little Janet is waiting to see you.'

Matron ushers him out of her office and into the visitor's room, where a little girl in a yellow dress stands, her double bouncing from the glassy floor. She calls him Daddy and asks him if they are going home now to see her mummy. He reaches out and gently touches her head. There are still no words. Even though they scream and rush at him from around the room, there are none which can lodge in his throat. None that can be uttered. Thoughts flit in and out of his mind. Janet looks so beautiful. So perfect. Then he notices, with a sudden stab of rage, that her thick golden plaits are gone. His pain becomes an aching, silent roar that engulfs him as she reaches up. His arms remember the shape of an embrace. They cling, their bodies dissolving one into the other seeking the warmth and reassurance and enduring love they had both once shared.

The little girl in yellow holds tightly to this man whose body shudders, and whose tears soak into the yellow bow and drip through her hair. The harder she cleaves, the less substance she feels. The bony frame dissolves. This man who is her daddy doesn't speak. His arms become lead. He turns and shuffles away out of the door. This ghost person, who leaves no trace of himself behind.

Accompanying him to the door, Matron speaks soothingly as she informs Bob that Billy has been moved to another home. 'A little bit further away, Mr Marshall. We feel that it's for his own good. He needs something more specialised than we can provide here.'

Fred and his wife drop him at his front gate. They are both concerned about his state of mind.

'Might just need a good night's sleep,' suggests Fred's wife.

Tinkling Water

'The attitudes of staff to children set the tone of the
environment in which they lived…the person in charge
had the power of total disposition of inmates and the
power to make their lives bearable or not.'
Forgotten Australians

Stony. That's how many of her work colleagues might have described her. Others might have said cold. Margaret is well into her forties now, grown stout with hair that has lost its coppery shine and rosewater perfume. It is cut short and is rather unbecoming. She trims it herself with the dressmaking scissors. Her starched white uniform, veil and sensible lace-up shoes indicate the practical, emotionally distant woman she has become.

She shoulders heavy responsibilities. The care and protection of her charges: more than two hundred children without homes or families. Sweetness and sentimentality are not requisites for such a task. For years, she has kept a tight rein on all aspects of managing such an enterprise, particularly the budget constraints. The laundry, which is a commercial operation, brings in good income and she feels a degree of satisfaction about this achievement. She finds the children exhausting and mostly unruly. The routines and disciplinary measures she has in place do at least minimise the disruption but there are always individuals who test her beyond the limit of her patience.

If she had been a mother, perhaps children would appeal to her more. Those maternal instincts she hears of might have guaranteed a smooth transition from maidenhood to motherhood and she would have probably have been surrounded by a brood by now. And her Tim would have been a marvellous father. He had such a sense of humour.

In the privacy of her room, there are occasional tears as she remembers that larrikin called Tim. His face is just shadows in her mind now and she needs to look at the black and white photo they had taken just before he signed up. They are both laughing their heads off at something silly but she can't remember what. A Tiffany lamp lights up the image. The lamp's brilliant colours are just as beautiful as on the very first day she brought it home. It remains bright and hopeful in a way she has not. A carved nubile figure balances the shade. Slightly risqué but her pride and joy all those years ago when she made the final payment to old Mr Green in the Hay Street antique shop.

'You've got a bargain there, my dear,' he'd said. 'A lovely Art Nouveau piece.'

She's still got the letter, from so long ago, that captured her dreams for their future.

Monday 23 March 1942

My darling Tim

Once again, I am waiting patiently for your letters which seem to arrive at odd intervals and sometimes several at once. Please do not think I am complaining. Quite the opposite, in fact. It is my habit to carry your latest letter with me and reread it constantly until I receive a new one. That way, I feel you are always close by.

I have some exciting news. Remember I told you that I'd seen a beautiful Tiffany lamp in an antique shop? Today I made the final payment. It is ours, my dear, and I feel sure you will love it as much as I do. The colours of the stained glass are quite stunning and I think it will complement whatever furnishings we choose for our future home.

This week has been very busy with an outbreak of influenza filling up the beds. We also get new polio patients most weeks. Very sad for some of the little children, who will be cripples for life.

I must sign off now, my love. The bathroom is finally free. Let's hope there is still some hot water for my bath. Always remember that I love you and I long for the day when we will be reunited.

Your loving fiancée

Maggie

She'd been a good nurse. The matron had complimented her efficient yet compassionate manner. Her pretty hair and shapely figure brought a smile to the faces of bed-bound patients. But after Tim, she'd turned inward. The warmth seeped out of her to be replaced by a coolness that eventually became glacial.

She made the change from hospital work to managing the children's home because it offered security, comfortable lodgings and no night duty. The once-beautiful old home was positioned in extensive grounds and, although run-down, there was still evidence of a lovely garden. With strong stewardship, she believed she could return the garden to its former splendour.

On her first day, rows of silent children were arrayed. They were ordered according to size and age. Standing with her feet planted apart in front of what she thought was a motley-looking bunch, Matron introduced herself. There was no whispering or shuffling. At least they seemed to be disciplined, she thought. Her preference was for silence during the day. Only at night did she enjoy the sound of beautiful and sometimes passionate music.

Passion might seem at odds with this terse, middle-aged woman. But once there had been a fervency in the letters she had continued to send to her far away fiancé. And those precious few letters she received in reply spoke of a reciprocal ardour. From the beginning, Tim's letters were full of optimism, discreet passion, even lyrical moments. She'd waved him off in Fremantle aboard the troopship *Queen Mary*.

His first letter had arrived about a month later.

7 February 1941

My dearest Maggie,

We have been sailing nearly two weeks now and are all feeling keen to get into the fray and on with job ahead of us. None of us know quite where we are but must be around the equator as the heat and humidity is pretty intense. Plenty of fun on deck with tug of war competitions. I've been on the winning team each time. Then we have a good salt-water wash down afterwards to cool off. I've met a lot of good blokes and we have plenty of laughs. The food is quite good. I suppose everything will change when we disembark. Bully-beef and tea might be all we get. I'm not sure when I will next get a chance to send mail so I hope this finds you well, my darling.

I do miss you and often dream about the special touch of your hair. Its feathery tingling against my neck. Its gentle hint of rose water filling my senses. Here's hoping this wretched war will be over soon and I'll be back with you all.

Stay safe, my darling.

Your loving fiancé,

Tim

But the letters became sporadic and sometimes contained so many blacked-out lines that it was difficult for Margaret to make much sense of them at all.

19 February 1942

Dearest Maggie

We are presently travelling in a convoy of troopships to an undisclosed destination. The men are exhausted but we are all endeavouring to keep our spirits up. I received the comfort parcel last week. The socks are very welcome.

I think of you daily and have your photo with me always. Some of the boys said that we might be home by the end of the year. How wonderful that would be.

Love forever, my darling,

Tim

Over the next year, a few more censored fragments reached Margaret. Then all correspondence ceased. Eventually, a letter-card declared that he was a prisoner of war at Sandakan POW camp somewhere in Borneo. His mother's neatly made-up face crumpled as she read the scribbled twenty-four words allowed by his Japanese captors. As the red lips pleated and quivered, Margaret's heart lurched. Her future mother-in-law could utter no sounds as she passed the dog-eared card to Margaret. It was a

Friday afternoon on one of those scorching summer days when the sea breeze refused to materialise. They were having their weekly cuppa on the front porch, hoping for a breath of cool air. Neither could articulate the rising dread that coursed in dark waves within them. They stared sightlessly over the box hedge stirring the tepid tea.

There were no more letters from Tim and, although she wrote wistfully, her instincts eventually told her that they never reached him. As the years passed, she steeled herself against the worst. There was no certainty that he was even alive. Eventually, the gruesome destruction came to an end. Armistice was declared and a telegram arrived. It was from Tim.

> Dear family,
>   I am safe. Being processed on hospital ship. Fed, washed, new uniform, rotten teeth pulled out. Waiting for evacuation ship.
>   Soon be on home soil.
>   Tim

His parents were overjoyed. Margaret's disbelief gradually faded. It was real. Her Tim was finally coming home.

'You just get yourself off to the dressmaker, my girl,' his mother instructed. Not normally a woman to blaspheme, her language escaped propriety. 'To hell with the expense! Order whatever you fancy. This will be a very special wedding.'

The man she met at the Fremantle wharf bore no resemblance to the robust, sandy-haired boy she had agreed to marry. The once-thick mop of hair was reduced to a few lank strands, the strong tradesman's shoulders were withered and stooped. Muscle had atrophied and only bone had survived. The skin resembled an old suitcase.

But it was the eyes that belonged to someone else. Tim's eyes were blue. That kind of summer sky-blue offset by a deep tan. Eyes that spoke of *joie de vivre* and daft jokes. This man's eyes were empty pools sealed below a faded blue-grey surface. A surface with no ripples, no reflections, no life. Empty, empty, spaces in a face Margaret no longer knew.

He went home to his parents to gain strength, to learn how to sleep, to become Tim. Even his mother's roast mutton and mint sauce couldn't tempt him. His body had lost its senses. Textures, aromas, flavours bounced off his leathery casing. Colour leached away, leaving him in a world of jagged grey shapes and surfaces.

After several months, he was sent to the country to stay with a distant cousin. The fresh air and farm life would hasten the healing. Banish the nightmares and sweats which recurred as he staggered through the jungle on that ghastly death march again and again and again. He took the gun to get a few rabbits. There were thousands of the buggers in the wheat belt.

Stan, the cousin, rang Margaret with the news. They'd found him up near the old dam. The top of his head, along with his hat, was gone.

The end of another long day. The quiet and seclusion of her room beckons, as does the contents of the bottle which dances in coloured lozenges under the lamp. Her room is situated at the far end of the second-storey wing. The dormitories are at the other end of the long passageway. After her bath, she returns to the room where a tray of supper has been placed near the door. Cold mutton, cheese, pickles and bread. And plenty of custard and pudding which Cook makes for the staff every day. Matron savours these sweet offerings. The room is comfortable and there is a small electric ring in the corner so she can make herself a pot of tea when she pleases.

But it's not tea she craves now. As she reaches for the bottle, her dressing gown falls open on pendulous breasts finally freed from a sensible and robust brassiere. Like Matron, the dressing gown has faded with the years. It was once a glorious fuchsia reflecting a romantic young woman who purchased it in the lingerie department of Boans department store. She settles into the armchair and tunes into ABC radio. A recording of Chopin's *Fantaisie Impromptu*, Opus 66, is being aired. The years of piano lessons flood back as she listens. A sense of melancholy pervades. She was a gifted pupil but earning any sort of income as a pianist was a ridiculous idea. Her mother had made that quite clear. Nursing had proven a practical and useful occupation.

Like water. That's how many had described Chopin's piano music. It travelled in tinkling cascades and sounded effortless, although she knew otherwise. She had attempted some of his better known works and had never mastered them completely.

She is transported away from the imposing walls of the children's home. Beyond the impressive gates and back to a place of green ferns and dappled sunlight. A cool veranda where a wicker table is set for afternoon tea. She is sixteen and along with two other young ladies is a guest of her piano teacher Mme Boulant. Madame is a cultivated woman whose presence sent tongues wagging years earlier when she arrived in Perth wearing a long fur coat and milky pearls. A grand piano followed her and she began giving lessons immediately. Her private life remained a mystery but it was acknowledged that she was a talented pianist and wonderful teacher. Margaret worshipped her and, as one of her best pupils, was invited to these intimate occasional gatherings.

The music splashes over her as she pulls the dressing gown tighter, closes her eyes and recalls that naïve young girl.

'Marguerette,' Madame always pronounced her name in a European way, 'I am so, so pleased with the way you are interpreting the Chopin. You have a very beautiful touch. Quite a gift young lady. Perhaps your mother will allow you to continue lessons for another year or so? Yes?'

'I don't think so, Madame. She says I need to get out to work. Anyway, if I get into nursing, I won't have a piano to practise on.'

'A pity, but we will see. Perhaps we can persuade her. Do have another éclair. I must watch my waistline.'

The fragile choux pastry crumbles into her mouth. It is the nearest thing to ecstasy she has ever experienced.

Madame pours more tea into the delicate bone china. The edge is rimmed in gold. Margaret's family has functional cream dinnerware, a world away from Madame's furs and pearls and grand piano. This other world is intoxicating yet out of reach, regardless of talent. Nursing is a sensible option and Margaret dutifully accedes to her mother's wishes.

'Matron! Are you there, Matron?' The door heaving under urgent hammering. 'Sorry to disturb you, Matron, but that Lyn Marshall and Beth Winsom have run away again. They must have sneaked out the gates when the doctor left.'

It's eleven p.m. by the time Margaret is in her uniform and back in the big hall. The police have been notified and the night staff are assembled. The empty beds were discovered half an hour earlier.

'Get them all out of bed and down here. At once.' Matron's face is as thunderous as her voice.

Rows of cowering, shivering girls ranging in ages from five to sixteen fill the hall by the time the police return the runaways. The rain has been heavy. The offenders are drenched and trembling as they are shoved onto the dais in front of Matron. As instructed, another staff member peels wet clothes from skinny bodies as Matron looms over them with her cane. The beating is ferocious and the welts create geometric designs as they ooze blood. The screaming bounces off the high ceilings and panelled walls. The sobbing and snivelling along the rows provides another layer of sound.

Matron's fury is finally spent and the two girls are shoved into the cupboard under the stairs. Their soaking clothes are tossed in with them.

'Back to the dormitories, all of you,' she barks. 'And let that be a lesson to any other girls who think that they can break the rules.'

The Chopin has finished and Wagner's *Valkyrie* is playing. Passion, fury, violence and destruction crash through her room. She reaches for the bottle shimmering under the suggestive lampshade. The whiskey catches in her throat for an instant. Her eyes close as the magic roars through her veins. Her hand reaches for the tattered fragment of a letter in the pocket of her gown.

Life is not all tinkling water.

For a Good Cause

'Among all the vividly recalled bad memories of life in an
institution, some also recalled happier occasions. Some...
institutions would provide an annual outing...'
Forgotten Australians

Never too much trouble

She was a good sort and actively charitable. As president of the
Dalkeith Ladies Society, there was the looming Orphans' Christmas
Party to arrange. It was always a big job and Mrs Taylor-Brown was not
one to take short cuts. The weather had been scorchingly hot, the kind
of summer that Diedre (for that was Mrs Taylor-Brown's first given
name) could do without, frankly. But this was Perth and for those
too far from the coast to benefit from the cooling Fremantle doctor,
the heat could remain most oppressive, even after sunset. Fortunately,
Diedre was not one of those unfortunates, her home being only a few
miles from the coast, with the added advantage of overlooking the
expansive Swan River, one of the city's most magnificent features. And
of course the most recent home improvement was the air conditioning
unit, which was a Godsend.

One of Diedre's friends, Flora, had recently moved to the foothills,
a dry, low escarpment many miles from the coast, where for the past
week the temperatures have hovered around the century. Diedre
wondered at the sense of this move to a location where there was never
a sea breeze, the flies were intolerable, and establishing a decent rose
bed was almost impossible. It wasn't her cup of tea at all.

Diedre often reminded herself of her comfortable, tasteful circumstances and was pleased to give her time generously to those less fortunate.

She had already run through her list today to check off the

Christmas party tasks. Sir James Wigmore had agreed to officiate, although she did find him a tremendous bore and she couldn't imagine why he had received a knighthood. Something to do with service in India, she'd heard. The afternoon tea committee will need reminding that Sir James would expect a tipple or two before the speeches. Also checked off her list were hiring table cloths; organising volunteers for gift wrapping; purchasing balloons and string; borrowing trestle tables from the tennis club; ordering sandwiches, cakes, ice cream and fruit cordial for the kiddies; plus of course the tea urn and crockery for afternoon tea. She was feeling a trifle overwhelmed with all these last-minute details but was reassured that she possessed the character and grit to carry on, despite the fact that she had felt rather out of sorts lately. Last on her list was the phone call to Elsie Trumpet.

Dear friends

It was always relief to let off steam with a special friend and Elsie Trumpet was a good listener. Diedre trusted Elsie and they telephoned one another most days just for a reassuring chat. This evening's call was to remark on the heat and to remind Elsie of her promise to attend the Christmas party although she wasn't a member of the Dalkeith Ladies Society. Elsie preferred the Canine Society and took great pleasure in presenting her furry children at the various shows. She was modest and rarely boasted about the trunk full of ribbons, mostly blue, that her precious boys had won.

After exchanging platitudes and forecasting a cool change, the subject of the Christmas party was broached. Diedre was counting on her friend to attend as moral support more than anything else. As she disclosed discreetly to Elsie, her irritation with the tedium of Sir James's monologues required a foil, and Elsie was that escape route. She would come to the rescue on an agreed cue. Diedre would catch her eye, wave and excuse herself graciously. Diedre expounded on some of the party details: the charming new doctor had agreed to be Father Christmas; the gift donations had been marvellously successful with over two hundred beautifully wrapped items; the newest ice cream flavour had been ordered – neapolitan, three different-flavoured layers – and, no, Elsie needn't be there until two p.m., when the children arrived on the buses. That would give her plenty of time beforehand to walk her pooches at the park. Elsie, as ever, was admiring of her friend's generous charity work. Diedre was a woman with a true Christian soul, she said, and Diedre felt uplifted by such approval. It made it all worthwhile.

She glanced out of the bay window and quietly marvelled at the splendour of this year's roses. The full (voluptuous really) heads stood defiantly through the summer heat. They needed plenty of water, of course, and the fowl manure kept them vigorous. Her mind, as her eye, wandered a little before coming back to the subject of the party, specifically the location. She explained that the Melrose family were hosting the party this year, a perfect setting with their spacious lawn tennis court and leafy gardens.

Farewells concluded, Diedre replaced the telephone earpiece in its cradle, smoothed the skirt of her lemon-coloured sundress and wandered out onto the patio for drinks with her husband, Teddy.

Gin and tonic

Teddy was a good man and had remained a most suitable husband. She'd been lucky. He had never strayed, was always sociable, and held his drink admirably. As a successful lawyer, he had provided wonderfully and was never mean with money. He still had a good head of hair, elegantly silvered, and a fine posture with little evidence of portliness. The boys had followed their father into law and shared his dark, good looks. They were both living nearby with quite pleasant wives and small children. Teddy had retired several years ago and spent quite a lot of his time at the golf club, which Diedre stoically declared was very good for his health. He also enjoyed the garden and was very particular about the roses.

It was the glorious result of his meticulous manicuring which was now on display. The adjacent north-facing patio was paved with limestone blocks and furnished with a white wrought-iron table setting. The upholstered chair covers were patterned with deep magenta roses mirroring the real blooms nearby. Gin and tonics were already on the table and Teddy had gone back to the kitchen for a bowl of nuts.

They had a woman who came in several times a week. She managed the cleaning and laundry and always prepared some of the evening meals. Diedre was rather a good cook, but was glad to escape the everyday routine. This evening, there was a piece of baked haddock with lemon sauce warming in the oven with a crisp salad in Diedre's favourite crystal bowl cooling on the refrigerator shelf.

Diedre breathed in the intoxicating perfume and swooned slightly as she waited for Teddy and the nuts. She had showered and changed before making the phone call to Elsie and her pale frock fell crisply just below the knees. Her legs were enclosed in the sheerest of stockings and her low-heeled court shoes were this season's tan and white. The weekly colour rinses had conserved the light chestnut of Diedre's hair and her skin showed minimal sun damage. She enjoyed tennis and at fifty-five remained trim and well preserved; not pretty exactly, but certainly still attractive.

'Busy day, Deedle-dum?'

'Exhausting, darling. And in this heat so much more trying. But at least by this time next week, it will all be over and I can rest up. Thank you for the drink Teddy-bear. A lifesaver, I'm sure.'

As the sun set and the squabbling parrots settled for the night, Teddy and Diedre enjoyed their icy gin and tonics generously flavoured with slices of lemon from the backyard tree. All things considered, Diedre thought life to be very satisfactory.

Party day

Diedre rose early and was fretful during the morning as she phoned various committee members, checking that all was under control. She had a touch of a head so she took some aspirin before leaving the house. Her relentless stewardship meant that by the time she arrived at the Melrose home soon after noon, everything looked in perfect order. The weather had been kind and a light sea breeze drifted across the cool lawns. Diedre checked and double-checked each trestle table as she greeted the ladies manning the various stations around the garden. She looked most becoming in a fresh chiffon flower-print frock with a matching pillbox hat. She was wary of large-brimmed hats at such occasions. Even a moderate breeze could unsettle such an accessory. Her gloves and shoes were a berry shade, complementing the same hue found in the print of her outfit.

She spotted Elsie, who had arrived earlier than anticipated. Diedre was quietly grateful for this slight change in arrangements. She embraced her friend warmly. 'Elsie, my dear, so lovely to see you. Are the doggies well?'

The two women moved to the edge of the garden to take in the vista, although not before Diedre had remarked on Elsie's striking hat. It had a broad, soft straw-like brim topped with two enormous silk roses.

'I must say that hat is absolutely stunning. Where on earth did you find it?'

'Bon Marche, my dear. They were having a sale and I fell for it, although I am a little apprehensive that it may be more suitable for a younger woman.' Elsie twirled in a rather girlish fashion to show its various facets.

'Don't be silly, Elsie. The colour of the roses is enchanting. So kind to your complexion.'

Diedre did have her doubts about its suitability for a woman of Elsie's age. It was almost an overstatement. But that was neither here nor there at the moment. She must press on with overseeing the occasion. She rather wished that Teddy was at her side but he had a competition day and Diedre had insisted that he carry on as usual. She could manage perfectly well and would be home by five.

She swallowed some more aspirin with a hurried cup of tea before moving to the front gate to greet Sir James. His face was already flushed as he scrambled rather awkwardly from the car, but he took a moment to gather himself before grasping Diedre's extended berry-encased hand with great vigour.

'Delighted, Mrs Taylor-Brown. How charming you look today,' he gushed.

This was not their first meeting. They both did the rounds of the various functions in Perth. It was mostly the same crowd. There were seldom surprises.

'On behalf of the Dalkeith Ladies Society, a warm welcome, Sir James. It is most generous of you to make time to join us today. Of course it is one of our most important events and we do think that it is imperative to show support for the good souls caring for these orphans.' Diedre was at her finest.

Sir James began what she knew was to come. A waffling, self-important diatribe on topics plucked at random from his woolly head. His florid face and slightly mumbled enunciation indicated that he had topped up the tank before leaving home. He rocked on his heels, clasped his hands behind his back and thrust out his bulging belly. Diedre smiled bravely for as long as she could endure before waving Elsie over to join them.

'I'll just get you something to clear the throat before the speeches,' she offered and hurried to the tea station where the ladies had discreetly hidden a fine malt whiskey.

She found a deckchair and settled Sir James under an umbrella near the little stage. He beamed benevolently about him as the potion worked its magic.

Diedre took a moment to catch her breath and surveyed the garden beds that were at their best for the occasion. The colours were superb and she felt a momentary flash of envy. The Melroses were very well heeled and employed a gardener almost full-time. Perhaps she and Teddy could afford one part-time. It would be rather fun to redesign some of the beds. She must ask Teddy about it when she got home.

But needs must and after her brief reverie, she was summoned to meet the buses that had just arrived.

The children dutifully filed down the steps in silence and stood in neat lines on the lawn. They were tidily turned out. A credit to those in charge.

'How pleasant to see you again, Matron. It hardly seems that a whole year has passed since our last orphans' party. Do come and meet Sir James before we get the afternoon's proceedings under way.'

Matron appeared dour. Large and imposing in the crisp white uniform and veil, Diedre had forgotten her cheerless aura. However, Diedre was skilled in bright conversation, albeit one-sided. Matron had little to contribute.

'Let me congratulate you on how beautifully turned out the children are, Matron. Some of those little frocks on the girls are very fetching indeed. Rather quaint, but most suitable, I'm sure. I suppose you must get some quite good things from jumble sales.'

Matron's face worked to shape the tiniest of smiles.

Diedre pressed on. 'Do allow me to show you around. Over here, we have the trestles with sandwiches and little cakes. Here is the fruit cup cordial. And afterwards we have an ice cream cone for each of them. Dr Whiteman is our Father Christmas this year. A wonderful Christian man if ever there was one. He will be distributing the beautiful collection of gifts which I am sure will bring joy to the poor little souls. And to finish the afternoon, we have organised some lively games.'

The afternoon proceeded smoothly and by the time the bus carrying Matron and the children had disappeared down the drive, Diedre was exhausted but gratified. It had all gone exactly as she had planned. She collapsed into a deckchair with a cup of scalding tea and swallowed two aspirin to ward off the nagging head. Returning home to free her puffy feet from their soft leather bindings was appealing.

Reflections

Feeling slightly refreshed, Diedre noticed Elsie assisting with the afternoon tea things. She waved her over to an adjoining deckchair. 'No need to do that, dear. The ladies have got it all in hand. Sit down and have a cup of tea.'

Elsie was still resplendent in her marvellous hat although, like Diedre, she had removed her gloves. She graciously accepted the teacup offered by one of the auxiliary ladies.

'I feel it all went very well and it was wonderful to see how delighted the children were with their gifts.'

'A marvellous success,' enthused Elsie.

'Thank you, Elsie.' Diedre smiled warmly at her friend before adding, 'And the kiddies seemed well behaved. Rather quiet really. None of that high-pitched clatter that can be so wearying.'

This lack of childhood clamour suited Diedre, whose conversational talents did not stretch to conversing with children. She didn't really see the necessity.

'Of course, I'm not saying for one moment that such qualities are not admirable. One thing I cannot abide is a chattering child. A sign of bad manners, I believe. I was just talking to Madge Fiddler. You know her, don't you, dear? She's a member of the Bridge Club. Anyway, Madge told me of a distressing experience she had recently when she attended a Red Cross luncheon where half a dozen boys and girls from the local high school had been invited. I can't imagine the purpose but the point is they had no idea of common table etiquette. I sometimes wonder about the kind of upbringing those types of families provide.'

A job well done

When Diedre arrived home, Teddy's car was already in the garage. He must have forgone drinks at the clubhouse. She let herself into the house and found him in the kitchen making himself a cup of tea.

'Hello, old thing. Like a cup of tea?'

'No thank you, dear. I had one just before I left the party. It went splendidly, I'm pleased to say.'

Diedre sat herself at the kitchen table and eased her burning feet out of her shoes. 'What a relief,' she breathed, stretching her legs under the table. 'Sir James expressed how impressed he was and just as he was leaving mentioned that we would be included on the guest list for the Governor's garden party next month. Isn't that a coup? It means that I will have to get straight over to the dressmaker. Just by chance, I saw a lovely lilac fabric in David Jones last week which might be very suitable.'

Diedre had noticed some most elegant new *Vogue* patterns and was keen to try one out.

'Good for you, Deedles. Some recognition for your hard work.'

Diedre needed to debrief a little. Like Elsie, Teddy was a good listener. 'The children were quite well behaved, which is a credit to those hard-working people who give their life to care for them. The gifts were so prettily wrapped. although some of the kiddies didn't seem to realise that they could keep the gift. There was one little girl aged about nine or ten, quite a plain little thing with glasses, who seemed particularly pleased with her present. It was a doll in a very sweet blue outfit that Mrs Roberts had donated. A pleasant woman actually, although she doesn't mix with our crowd very much. I think she must be involved in the Musical Society. She plays the piano rather well, I've heard. Anyway, this child seemed fond of the doll right away and sat on the lawn talking to it all afternoon. Completely absorbed in her own world. I suppose you can't be sure what goes on in these children's heads. Not very savoury backgrounds most of them, it seems. Matron suggested, quite discreetly I will say, that not many are orphans after all. I was most surprised at that and it does set you thinking about what sort of parents would abandon their own flesh and blood.'

Diedre's head was beginning to nag again. 'I'm just going to have a little lie down, Teddy. Wake me for drinks, dear.'

A soul at rest

Teddy looked frightful. The shock had not only drained every vestige of colour from him, it seemed to have diminished him entirely. He shuffled like a man two decades older as he made his way to the front pew. There was a big crowd. Diedre had been a stalwart of the community and her sudden and unexpected passing had shocked them all to the core. As Elsie had explained as she bravely phoned one after another, Deidre Anne Taylor-Brown had suffered a massive stroke on the very day she had so magnificently hosted the orphans' christmas party. Poor, dear Teddy had poured the drinks and gone to rouse her after a nap. Nothing could be done. She was gone even before arriving at the hospital.

Charles, a close friend of the family, delivered the eulogy, reminding the weeping mourners of her extraordinary contribution to charitable works. His voice was oratorical.

No One Was Watching

'There was no surety that any child who passed through
the gates of an institution would not suffer psychological,
physical or sexual violence, because no-one was watching.'
Inside: Life in Children's Homes and Institutions

A thud on the back of my neck as I walk through the yard. It's the shock that unbalances me and nearly sends me sprawling. I'm not as steady on my pins as I once was.

Bloody hell! What was that?

Just a little welcome gift, the screw says.

His sneer is as dark and hard as the bitumen leading to Block A. High supervision.

Nothing they hate more than a paedophile. They'll have plenty of names for you, mate. Rock spider. Kiddy jumper. Yeah. That's why we'll keep an eye on you. Just till you settle in.

The warm oozes under the collar of my regulation shirt and trickles down my back. Thick like treacle. But I still don't get it. Until the stench smothers me and I gag. Turning in a circle like a bloody dog chasing its tail. Trying to get away from the stink and the slime.

Now I'm in here I've got all the time in the world to pick through the past and try to put together some sort of a story about what the hell this is all about. You know that I was never much of a talker. Always kept things to myself pretty much. I thought I might write it down for you to read – you know how we used to leave notes for each other? But longer, more like a letter. I'm pretty sure that where you are you might already be able to read my mind, but writing it down might help me make some sense of it. And just to get things straight, I'm not here at Her Majesty's pleasure. That's for the ones they reckon are insane and or at high risk as a repeat offender. My sentence is what the judge said was 'a reflection of the seriousness of my crime and the community's expectation that child molesters should be punished harshly'. Seven years is what he gave me. It could be worse, I suppose. In some states, it's life now. So my sentence can be measured and the days crossed off. I've got acres of time to study the smoothness of the walls in my 7.5-metre box. No necks can be stretched in here unless it's another pair of hands doing the stretching. Which I'm beginning to realise isn't so unlikely. Functional, hygienic steel and concrete that can be hosed to remove unsightly stains. Bells signal routines to remind me of day and night. Sirens scream warnings of threatened mutiny and silent violence.

I can tell you, Thelma, I'm getting a feel for the place pretty quickly. After the first few weeks, the threats and abuse made it clear to me that I was clinging to the lowest rung of the prison ladder. My fellow inmates muttered at me that I was just a fuckin' rock spider who was always looking for little cracks to crawl into. A filthy prick, they called me. I'm not sure if that's what you thought. Maybe it was and that's why you stopped talking.

But that's the way it is here. Worse than them, they reckon. Which is a laugh if you're in the mood. Brutal criminals most of them. Wife-bashers, thugs, thieves, drug-pushers, rapists, murderers. Animals and useless layabouts who've probably never done an honest day's work. Covered in disgusting tattoos. Bulging bellies, missing teeth, spitting and swearing as they stake out their territories. There's no way I'm one of them. I worked in a white-collar job. Wore a suit and tie to work and had a first-class ticket on the train. A responsible married man who always brought home an honest wage. You'd have to agree with that, Thelma, even though the drink was a slight problem at times.

I'm not one of those animals. Not even close.

I've been on high supervision since I've been inside. My exercise time is before the rest of them. Just to walk around the quadrangle and get a breath of fresh air. Listen to a few bird calls, which settles me. I can usually identify some species that I check in my bird book when I go back in.

But that's coming to an end. The guard informed me that I was going out with the rest of them tomorrow. He couldn't disguise the smirk in his voice as he told me that I'd have to take my chances. Which, he knows as well as me, are not too good. Bastard.

'Inside' is a just another war zone when I think about it. Adrenalin keeps you on high alert. You start jumping at your own shadow and you never turn your back. The screws are mostly blind and deaf. The stink of piss and shit and blood and fear fills the air. The nightmares are already getting to me: night after night with sounds and smells and broken bodies. And this is just the beginning. Six years, nine months, four days to go. I might get out early for good behaviour and completing all the courses for 'crims' like me. What do think my chances are, Thelma? Remember when I did that course for work? Safety-first stuff – load of bullshit really – but I topped the class. You know as well as anyone that I'm not stupid, so I reckon I'll give all the programmes my best shot.

I'll admit that it was a bloody mistake but I thought it was over and done with. I feel like it was something that happened to some other bloke a million years ago. And I reckon it would have happened to plenty of other blokes back then. In those days, you kept your business to yourself and just got on with life. Blokes made mistakes and urges overpowered common sense sometimes but people never used to make such a fuss about things like that. I put the whole episode to the back of my mind and the details are hazy and fragmented. How can I remember what the kid might have felt like? She was just a kid and kept her mouth shut just like any other kid. But it turns out that she never forgot and when they heard her story they tracked me down like a dog. Just one skinny kid who didn't kick up any fuss about it at the time. And it never happened again after she left.

When I saw her standing in the courtroom, it shocked the blazes out of me. I wouldn't have recognised her but there was something about her voice that took me back all those years. She was usually pretty quiet but I remember once when she'd baked a cake with you, Thelma, and she fairly trumpeted like an elephant as she took it out of the oven. It was that same voice in the courtroom as she pointed to me and boomed that I was Mr Victor White and that she'd been sent to live in our home when she was ten. She went on and on with her story, the details of which I had little recollection.

She'd always been so quiet. I would never have guessed that she'd have that in her.

I'll admit that I was glad you'd already gone, Thelma. I still believe that I was made a scapegoat but I know you wouldn't have coped too well with all the court business. And once the story came out, I understand that you would never have been able to face your church group. I'm retired now, so the blokes at work probably don't know about it, because I don't see them any more. There's no one really to point the finger, which is some sort of a blessing, I suppose. A man has to hang on to whatever dignity he can muster. Thank goodness we never had any kids. I'm not sure that I could have faced them after all this.

When I think back, I'm sorry that it affected you so much at the time. I remember you even threatened to leave but where would you have gone, Thelma? It wasn't adultery and I wasn't a wife-basher. You were always such a practical woman, so I was relieved when you seemed to accept that what was done couldn't be undone. Maybe it would have helped if we'd talked about it, but you were pretty determined not to talk at all. I thought you were overly hard in that way, Thelma, and I recall telling you to let bygones be bygones.

I was in the hallway putting on my hat, ready to leave for work. But you just scowled at me before you turned around and marched back to the kitchen. Funny, I can see that as clear as day. But you stuck to your guns. Not a bloody word. That's when I worked out the notebook system that we used. Until you went, actually. Seems strange – not a word in all those years.

Well, I'm still writing and the further back I look, the more I can see that you were always a pretty strong-willed woman. You used to nag and nag about having a kid but it was all too fast for my liking. We'd only been married a few months and it was on. I can still hear your voice as you sweet-talked me into early nights in bed. Then in the afterglow you talked more decidedly of baby prams, layettes and the colour of the nursery.

But I wasn't really up for it, Thelma. I was only just back from the war and had survived somehow in one piece. Better off than lots of blokes. Johnny Phillips with only one arm. Jack Winter with half a leg. Ted Jones with no nose and only one ear. That bloke Simon with a metal plate in his head and no one understanding a word he said. And poor bloody Peter Shepherd with his balls blown away. I knew that I was pretty lucky. None of us blokes ever talked about the war, even though there had been a few newspaper reports about the Australian troops in New Guinea. Mostly about major offensives like the Kokoda campaign. But so many of us were spread out all over the place fighting in remote jungle terrain battling the heat, biting insects, malaria and dysentery just as much as fighting the Japs. Even though I'd escaped that hellhole, there were times when half-remembered moments crashed over me like waves that knocked the stuffing out of me. Trying to settle back into civvy life wasn't so easy. Bed at night was a battlefield as sleep came and went. Remember, there were times when you had to roll to the edge of the bed as I tried to kick a hand grenade out of the way. I wasn't too confident about this having a kid so soon. I felt like I needed more time to settle back to normal. Back to the way things were before the war. And remember, getting married was your idea. I'd taken you to the pictures a couple of times and I thought you were a good sort. We had a kiss and cuddle when I dropped you home and suddenly you were full of wedding plans. I just went along with it. I can't say I'd thought about it much. But I was twenty-four and I did have a trade. Lots of my mates were married already, so it seemed like the right thing to do.

I know that you were pretty upset that the baby thing didn't work out. I don't know why the little buggers just kept slipping out. Did the doctor ever say why? Then when the last one was pretty far on, you went to pieces. I was pretty sorry about it all too but that was just how it was. At the back of my mind, I was almost relieved to be honest. My old man was such a nasty violent prick. I didn't have much of a clue about how a father should be. What if I'd turned out just as bad as he was? Luckily I didn't seem to have his temper and I never belted you the way he bashed Mum.

Actually, I was glad when you joined the church group. You seemed to brighten up with all the activities and meetings: jumble sales and baby clothes for the orphans. That kind of thing. I didn't even mind too much when you talked me into helping set up the trestle tables. I know I grumbled but I was pleased that you'd stopped sitting at the kitchen table just staring into space. It went on for months and I remember saying to you that you needed to get out more often.

But you just drank tea and the dripping tears went on like a leaky cistern.

If you think about it, Thelma, we were doing pretty well apart from the baby business. We had a war service house in Leederville and it wasn't too bad at all. Brick and tile with a few rose bushes in the front and plenty of room out the back for chooks and some vegies. And the geraniums you planted out the back brightened up the yard no end. Oh, I forgot: they weren't geraniums. You put me in my place about that, I remember. You were most insistent that they were pelargoniums.

I have to laugh when I recall you full of importance about the superior qualities of pelargoniums. Puffed up like one of those fat crested pigeons who strutted around the chook yard picking up odd wheat kernels. Not the same soft cooing, though. More like a galah. I used to feel unsettled when you were in full squawk but I learnt to block out the sound, otherwise it might have tipped me over the edge. Like old Charlie Butler who belted his wife with a leg of lamb. He reckoned it was her voice. Got ten years for it, poor bugger.

The train station was only a ten-minute walk, so getting to work and home again was plain sailing and I was pretty happy with my work. The blokes out there were a good lot mostly and didn't jibe me too much when I moved from a blue collar to a white collar job. Just like Dad, I was a fitter and turner but I'd done extra night classes and got promoted to order clerk. I was pleased as punch, if you want to know, and you seemed proud to see me off in the mornings in a suit and tie. I suppose that pelargoniums were more suited to our status.

It was about then that I'd sometimes stop off after work for a drink or two. The pub was handy – next door to the station. I'd down a few beers and have a chat with whoever was there. Mostly it was Simon and I'd have to remind him who I was but he always knew when it was his round, so I guess his mind wasn't altogether gone. I'm not too sure what he was on about but it filled the time if there was no one else to talk to.

By the time I got home, tea was on the table. We never had much to say to each other, except when you nagged about me having a quiet drink or two. I can remember that. You'd get all high and mighty about my drinking habits embarrassing you and how there were jobs waiting to be done in the yard and what Alice Croft had to say about men who drank at the pub.

I still claim that to have a yarn with the blokes over a few beers wasn't a crime. We always had money to pay for a roof over our head and food on the table. There was nothing to complain about and I reminded you that as head of the household it was my right to have a few drinks with my mates if I wanted to. I also think that the drink was a help for the nightmares. And it drowned out the ringing in my head. Some of the blokes called it shell shock. I don't know about that but it just went on and on. It still bothers me, if you want to know.

The writing seems to settle me, so I'll go on with the story, Thelma. I'm really stretching back into my memory now to figure out what happened next.

I recall you announcing that we should do something for the poor orphans from the home that the church group talked about. I didn't see the point myself. They had plenty of good people to look after them where they were. But you were quite vocal about it and you hardly talked about anything else. Looking back, I think it was when things really changed in our lives. It kind of took over everything. You just kept at me about how these poor little kiddies needed a real home and we had one with a spare bedroom and you could do with company and you'd heard at church that you could foster these kiddies if you were a good Christian family and of course we were because you went to church every week and it was pretty obvious that the house was clean and tidy because the vicar came for afternoon tea once a month and it was clear that I kept the front lawn in good order. And anyway it would be good to have a child who could help out around the house.

That's why Janet came to live with us. A bloody mistake if ever there was one.

It pains me now to think about all the fuss and bother we had to go to. We had to visit the home to look over the kiddies, although I did agree it was a good idea to choose one that seemed suitable. You wouldn't want to end up with some little runt who couldn't do a decent day's work. The home was in the hills, so I borrowed my brother-in-law's car for the day to make a kind of an outing of it and you were pretty excited about it all, what with a picnic lunch and Thermos flask. I remember that you made me wear my suit and you were dolled up in gloves and a hat. I thought it was too much but you kept saying that we had to make a good impression with the matron, otherwise they might not let us take one of the children.

You'll remember Ron had the car waiting for us on the Saturday morning. A beautiful vehicle, a Singer saloon that he'd bought second-hand but in tip-top order. Very roomy inside with a brown leather-covered bench seat and pull-down armrests. Real walnut dashboard as well. Even a heater and demister. I'd have to agree with you, Thelma, that the drive up to the hills was very pleasant. Quite relaxing, and when we found a shady spot off the edge of the road, we spread out the rug and had our egg sandwiches and Thermos of tea. I can still taste that jam sponge you'd made. I have to say you were a good cook. The muck we have in here reminds me of that every day.

When we got to the home gates, I was amazed at how enormous they were. Great iron things that reminded me of a prison (and I know all about that now). Matron was waiting for us on the front step and we followed her through the huge hallway into quite a grand reception room. I suppose you'd remember how stern Matron looked. Her stiff chest crackled as she walked and her shoes squeaked on the glassy polished floor. A real battleship sort. She greeted us and reminded us in a thunderous voice that the children could only go to good Christian families and that she must be sure we were suitable.

Then another woman in a nurse's uniform brought in a tray with a pot of tea and plate of biscuits. Matron poured. The cups were those little flowery things that hardly hold more than a mouthful and threaten to smash in your hands. I know that you commented on how delicate they were and seemed to enjoy sipping away with your little finger pointing to nowhere in particular. Anyway, it was obvious to me that these orphan kiddies had the best of everything here, so I hoped that if we took one of them, they wouldn't expect to be treated like royalty.

After the tea, Matron took us up to the playroom to see the children. It was another big room with a glossy floor and about a dozen girls playing with a range of very good-looking toys. They were aged from about six to eleven or twelve, I would guess. Very neatly turned out, all of them. Hair ribbons and polished shoes. You and Matron seemed to hit it off. They all looked the same to me, so I just waited for you to choose someone. I wasn't really taking much notice but Matron wanted to drag me into it. Her voice wasn't quite so booming. She seemed to approve of us and was almost charming as she pointed out a child with yellow ribbons who she considered might be suitable. The girl had been in the home for five years and at ten years of age Matron thought that she might be helpful around the house. Apparently she was a ward of state, so she was available for adoption if we so desired.

The whole thing was your idea, Thelma, and I don't believe that I had much say in the matter. But she seemed all right to me. Pretty quiet when she came back to Matron's office with us, but that was good as far as I was concerned. I was finding noisy women's chatter more and more irritating. So we took her. Signed a few forms and that was that. Matron handed us a small case and we all drove off.

So that was when it all began, I suppose. The part in the story when things really started to go wrong, although you couldn't have known that. Nor did I. You were so full of yourself back then.

You sounded like a bird crowing from the top of a tree as you prattled on about how we were a real family now.

Janet never said a word all the way home.

I didn't take much notice of her at first. Hardly heard a word out of her, to be honest. She was always out in the backyard sweeping or cleaning out the chook house or collecting kindling for the stove in the mornings when I went off to work. After school, there was always ironing and cooking to be done, so she kept out of sight mostly. You seemed to think that things were working out all right and the ladies at church were quite impressed, you said. You'd sometimes report to me about how much they commended your fine Christian spirit. About the generosity of such a gesture, despite all sorts of warnings they had heard about how unsuitable many of these children could be. Not knowing what kind of background they came from was hazardous, they suggested, but despite all that you were doing a wonderful job.

I could see that you were feeling quietly pleased with yourself when they fussed and clucked.

I remember how you used to keep her home from school on Mondays, because it was washing day. I can see now that must have been a big help, what with lighting the copper and the wringer and the starching.

And she wasn't a big eater, so it seemed that all in all things were working out quite well. As I said, I didn't see much of her but I had noticed that she was pretty skinny. Had long legs like a young filly. I must say I'd always liked the look of those long slim legs on a young girl. And once summer came, you made her some shorts to wear around the house. They certainly suited her and I began to watch her more often. Then I noticed that she was wearing shorty pyjamas that you'd made for her. Pink and white they were. They were what young girls wore those days. Instead of long nighties. Much cooler and more comfortable, you said. She used to put them on after her bath and sit in the kitchen to read before she went to bed.

So having Janet around the house wasn't causing any problems at that time.

I'm guessing that it must have been a few months later when my nightmares seemed to get worse. I would get up in the night and have another beer or two to settle myself. Janet would sometimes walk through the kitchen out to the toilet on the veranda while I was sitting at the table. She was always half asleep and never seemed to notice me there. It just happened from there really. I thought I'd just settle her back to bed. Those long legs were so smooth as I tucked her in, and the first time it happened without me thinking about it. I just wiped it up and she didn't say anything. Just lay still and quiet in her pink bed. Next time was the same. Never moved or made a sound. It just went on from there. I could hear her gasp and gulp at the air and her skinny body would go rigid but she didn't make any other noises. It was a distraction from the nightmares and I always slept well afterwards. She kept her mouth shut and sometimes I slipped a few lollies under her pillow. It was just between her and me. There was no harm intended. I would never have hurt her or anything. It was always over pretty quickly and she still had you fussing around her. Everything seemed to go on as usual.

Then that night you went off to bed early with a headache was when it all changed. My memory is fuzzy but I must have just stayed on in the kitchen having a few more drinks. Usually I only visited

Janet's room if the nightmares had woken me, but for some reason I slipped in there before going to bed. There was nothing different. She was as silent as always and I was just tidying myself up as I walked out of her room. And there you were standing in the hallway. I can't really remember what happened next. The shouting, doors banging, furniture crashing. It's all a blur of noise and movement. I just cleared out when you dragged her out of the bedroom with the stuff still running down her legs. I could hear you from the back porch: going berserk, belting the daylights out of her and screaming at her to pack her bags. Strangely, I remember feeling slight relief when I heard you telling her what a dirty, filthy creature she was. And I silently agreed with you about her going back to the home. It reassured me a little that you were probably quite right. Janet had seemed rather slinky as she walked past me in the kitchen.

My memory is clearer about that day when I got home from work. Janet was gone. You'd moved my clothes to the spare wardrobe and Janet's bed was freshly made up. The pink bedspread was gone. In its place was a dark green cover. Our bedroom door was shut. My tea was in the oven. That was when you stopped talking and I worked out the notebook system. The messages were short but never nasty, if I remember rightly. When to put the bins out, or mow the lawn or pay the milkman.

To be truthful, Thelma, I didn't mind it all that much and I began to listen for other sounds. We had plenty of visiting birds in the backyard and I enjoyed spending time with them. You might recall that I set up a feeding platform with seeds and water and built a wooden bench under the gum tree. Over those years, I began to recognise quite a range of species. Although I do realise that you didn't care much for the birds and I noticed a couple of times you had tipped their seeds into the bin. Even when you were sick, we kept the notebook going. I've no idea what you were thinking at that time. Or what the doctor said. I suppose that I thought you would be all right but maybe you knew otherwise. Anyway, when you'd gone, I enjoyed the birds even more.

Some of them screeched and squawked but oddly I never found their sounds unpleasant. Quite soothing, in fact.

It's been nearly twenty years since you passed on and, as I said before, I'm grateful that you haven't had to go through all this again. Now I've been thinking more about all this business, I can see that there were some particular facts about my situation. I think I was the victim of circumstances. Maybe the drink might have muddled my mind too but I can see a kind of pattern now I've written it down. Events that were out of my control all conspiring against me in the end. Maybe if I hadn't met you, none of it would have occurred. Not that I'm blaming you, Thelma. Just wondering about it, that's all.

I've been writing all night, Thelma. Once I got started, it wasn't too hard. I'm pretty tired but today the weather's beautiful. That mild autumn sunshine we get in Perth always lifts my spirits and the early morning birdsong I can hear from my cell fills my head. It's as though I'm transported from the humdrum of prison life with the chatter of willy-wagtails, shrieking parrots, twittering wrens and magpies' song; all exploding in fantastic colours inside my brain. Was today the day I'm going out with the rest of them? I don't seem to remember too clearly. Maybe it was next week.

When the screw comes to my cell, I remind him that I should have gone out before the others but he just grunts that he's had enough of watching over some pervert and he wouldn't be giving up his smoko time to let me go out after the others. It was time for the big event, he sneered. Nasty prick.

I'll stop writing for now. You probably already know all this stuff, but I think it's helped, so I'll write again to let you know how I go with the counselling courses. I know it might sound silly but I still believe that the dead can just look down and see everything that's happening. Can you do that, Thelma?

The guard is leaning against the smoko shed on the other side of the fence. He inhales slowly as the nicotine works its soothing magic. Eyes screwed up against the brilliant sky, he glances over to the exercise yard half watching the kiddy jumper stumble into the yard. He sniggers and spits into the dirt as he observes. Plenty of time. Smoko doesn't finish for another fifteen minutes.

The spider is clinging to the wall but the shadows flicker around and somehow circle him. Spitting and hissing that he's a fucking filthy paedo. Needs to be taught a few lessons, they jeer. Gobs of slime pelt down. Steaming piss splashing off his face as his hands rake at his eyes. Low chanting echoing off the corrugated smoko shed. Louder and louder, bouncing off the hot bitumen now. A sharp cracking sound breaking through the cacophony. Methodical thudding. Noises like tearing flesh and crunching bone.

Chip off the Old Block

> '…the use of corporal punishment was widespread, socially
> accepted and children were legally the chattels of their parents.'
> *Historical review of sexual offence and child abuse*
> *legislation in Australia: 1788–2013*

1917: For King and country

His mum is so proud. 'I always knew you could do it even though your father had nothing good to say about it.' She's beaming at him as he leans gawkily against the kitchen door frame.

'He took too much notice of that ridiculous report if you ask me,' she adds. 'Charlatan. That's what I reckon about that professor whatever-his name was.' She wrings her wet hands on her apron and hugs Walter before he can duck.

'Thanks, Mum.' Wal is embarrassed by her fussing but secretly proud as punch with having received his official papers.

A qualified fitter and turner. It's not such a bad trade. In his dreams, he'd imagined that he would be a clerk in a cushy job filling in ledgers. Inside work, warm and cosy with office girls you could chat up. But there's nothing wrong with honest manual work. Makes a man out you, everyone reckons, and Wal doesn't disagree. Anyway, he's not smart enough for all that figuring work, so no use wasting time worrying about it. In fact, that professor his mum mentioned had written that he needed to improve his memory of figures. He's never got around to it.

He's been at the workshop since he was fourteen. Nearly five years and although he hasn't told his mum yet, he's pretty keen to join the boys overseas and see something of the world. Now that he's finally completed his apprenticeship, he can enlist. He and a few mates have agreed to sign up after work. They're all as keen as mustard to be off on the adventure of a lifetime.

When he finally breaks the news, his mum is heart-broken.

'You're just a lad. Let the men fight wars,' she wails.

But, kitted out in their new uniforms, they are men. They laugh and skylark. Free at last from their mothers' niggling and fretting. The train journey across the Nullarbor to Victoria is one continuous caper. Changing trains, days and nights of travel, no one getting much sleep but no one caring. They're still buzzing with a mixture of fatigue and exhilaration as they board troopship *Aeneas*. It is 30 October 1917 as they sail out from Melbourne. A new world beckons.

Walter begins the letter home to his mother three days out of port. He adds to it every few days.

> … After being three days out we passed the north corner of New Zealand and we have not seen land since for eight days. Directly we passed New Zealand we struck a very rough beam sea & you ought to have seen them sick, I don't suppose there was more than 200 that were not sick…

He's delighted with what every day has to offer. Physical games most days, with tug-of-war and potato race competitions fiercely fought. He came third in the potato race and his crib game is really improving, he reports to his mother.

> …well, Mother, I have to play in a crib tournament tonight, I hope that I have better luck…

The concerts are a laugh. Always some comedian dressed up as a girl who brings the house down and his unit won the bass, baritone and tenor solos in the singing competition. He is particularly proud to tell his mother that he has managed the challenge of washing his own clothes but adds,

> …another washing day, I'll never be a bachelor after this lot it is too hard washing clothes…

By the end of a month at sea, the seventeen-page letter captures the thrill of sighting land, awe of passing through the Panama Canal, astonishment at the speed of the American navy motor launches and general excitement in everything from fire drills to rock cakes for dinner. Signing off, 'Your loving son Walter', it contains no evidence of trepidation. There is no mention of looming battlefields or impending death.

The scales fall

That seventeen-page letter home to his mum captured Walter's innocent sense of wonder. It was the promise of freedom and adventure that had lured him away from the strictures of a safe and conservative community. Of course, he'd heard that many boys from home had made the final sacrifice. But the sense of mateship and patriotism wiped out the shocking statistics along with the gruesome realities of war. The promise of escape from humdrum lives that offered little free time, an occasional few shillings to spare and no sex other than what you provided for yourself. The chance to get away from smothering mothers, domineering fathers, annoying brothers and sisters and never-ending work sounded a dream too good to be true. You got five shillings a day, which wasn't at all bad. The Poms only got one shilling a day when they joined. His mates had even heard that there was plenty of sex in exotic places. What more could a young fellow want?

It was to be the only letter he sent home. The ghastly reality of the trenches clogged his lungs as it killed his mates and any further literary inclinations. In just under two years, he was back home. The carnage was over and by some kind of miracle he was still alive. The four mates he'd enlisted with were gone. The gullible boy was a man with blood and guts and mud and stench and fear embedded in his being. Nightmares stalked him. And the coughing wore him out. The foul yellow gas had transformed him. He was a man much older than his years.

1922: A bun in the oven

Once home again, the Railways sent him off to Northam, sixty miles out of Perth. He lived in a boarding house and it wasn't too bad. Mrs Little cooked a good roast on Sundays and her daughter Gladys was quite a looker. He started to hang around the house more when he got home from work. Helped out with chopping the wood and lighting the copper. Mr Little was an invalid and couldn't do much. There wasn't a lot happening in town but once a month or so there would be dance down at the hall. The CWA ladies would make a bang-up supper and there was a keg on tap. Mrs Frances from down near the station played the piano and old Mr West would play the fiddle. So he asked Mrs Little (Mr Little was poorly again) if it would be all right for Gladys to come to the dance with him. Gladys was seventeen now and worked at the bakery. She seemed pretty keen, so off they went, her balanced on the handlebars as he wobbled the bicycle two miles to the hall.

He had to admit she looked a bit of all right and the other blokes gave some encouraging wolf whistles as they arrived. Her frock was what she called apricot and seemed to consist of miles of net and lace. It frothed around her rather shapely figure very attractively, if the truth be known. She had long gloves and he had bought her a corsage which just about broke the bank. It was what the florist called delicate; white baby's breath with a white rosebud in the middle.

Anyway, the dance was just the beginning. Things moved on from there quicker than he planned and before you knew it she was in the family way, which of course meant they had to get married pretty smartly to cover their tracks. Victor was born six months later, rather premature the story went, but a whopping ten pounds nonetheless.

Bloody Vic. Been a bundle of misery ever since he was born. Always crying. Hardly slept. Ears that stuck out like jug handles. Good thing he was born so fat because he just didn't thrive at all that first year or so. Always vomiting all over the place.

1926: Married life

'Bloody fool. You need to have your head read.' It's the wife muttering as she bashes her bottled fury into the pastry. 'Married life,' she spits.

He's just staggered in from the pub. 'What the hell did you say?' His lungs might be buggered but Wal's hearing is still pretty good.

Her response is methodical punching. The thudding sounds ricochet from the dark cavern of the kitchen.

'For God's sake, woman. Will you just leave off,' he slurs wearily. He shoves through the fly wire door and thumps up the path to the thunderbox for a scrap of peace and quiet.

Now he's out of the house, the kitchen, which had expanded to bursting, settles as the kneading becomes more meditative. She remembers that he had once. Had his head read. They'd both had a laugh about it when he'd found the Mental Science College chart in his father's belongings. Five bob his father had forked out in 1910. Wal was eleven years old. The phrenologist was a Professor A.J. Abbot, MRPS, who provided a full written report on the forty-three different faculties of the aforementioned boy, Walter Thomas White. The father had obviously believed this new science would prove worthy of the investment.

Number 42

Intuition: will judge character well.

His father was probably disappointed and aggrieved at wasting his five bob. The predictions deduced from his son's cranial bumps mostly proved inaccurate. Gladys had come to similar conclusions and the above attribute was a case in point. He was always off to see a bloke who knew a bloke who could make a quick quid. She'd never witnessed any money-making miracles and the bloke in question seemed to evaporate as quickly as he had appeared, usually with a pocket full of Wal's cash.

'Good judge of character, my fat aunt,' she grumbled.

Number 3

Bibativeness: not liable to inebriety.

'Now that is a joke,' she snorted.

Only ten minutes ago, Wal had reeled through the back door. The wage packet left on the kitchen table was lighter by half and Wal's wits were reduced by a similar fraction. He'd backed a sure thing.

In the dunny, what with the heat and the flies, Wal can't get comfortable. His head pounds. His guts broil. Jesus. What was a man to do with responsibilities looming over him like a toppling mountain? Two bloody kids and another one on the way. He was smothering under it all. He finally settles his skinny arse on the wooden seat.

'It's a battle for a bloke just to have a fag and a quiet read of the racing pages,' he mourns.

But after his bad luck, even the nags don't capture his interest much today. He gloomily reflects on how he had arrived in such a predicament and recalls that he'd been warned before he got married. Your life's not your own any more, his already married mates had predicted. They were bloody right. And even though he had savoured the goods beforehand, there had been a certain sense of abandon during the two-day honeymoon. But it wasn't long before the fleshy privileges had been restricted, eventually to tight rations. Headaches, woman's troubles and exhaustion were the cited excuses. It became apparent that she'd pretty much shut up shop not long into the marital enterprise and what for him had been the main benefit of the contract had been tacitly withdrawn.

He'd come to realise that there was no option but to take what was his right whenever the urge came. A few drinks helped him along. She bore the incidents in silence. Presumably thinking of England while he pumped away at her. What infuriated him was that she fell pregnant just having him in the same bed. Four times in the four years they'd been married. One didn't make it but that still left two with one more around the corner.

He tears off a square of newspaper and swipes at his bum.

Steering clear of the house, he settles on the chopping block at the wood heap. The lemon tree provides a cooling umbrella as he lights up.

He must have dozed off. The fag hanging in the corner of his mouth is all ash. Wal grinds the butt under his boot and sneaks past the kitchen. She must have popped next door to collect Vic and Ethel, who've been having a play with the neighbour's kids. Wal can't work out why but he's just never taken to Victor at all. He's a skinny little whiner who needs a backhander every so often. After Vic came Ethel and she has a sweet nature. Then they lost one. Another boy. Still waiting for the next and Wal hopes it's another girl. They seem to be easier and keep out of the way most of the time.

He's taken the rest of the racing pages out onto the front veranda and tucks himself in the cane chair behind the potted plants. With luck, he can stay out of sight until teatime. He can't face Victor's bleak dial.

1930: A sorry sight

The children were growing older. The girls were all right, but Victor continued to get under his skin. A runt of a kid really, with those bloody big ears and snivelling nose. Wal had always given him a hiding when he had messed things up. Or moped about with that long face of his. Vic was at school now and Wal could see that he needed some more smartening up if he was ever going to amount to any sort of a man. It was high time he had some sense knocked into him. And the time came soon enough. Walter saw red one afternoon as he caught sight of Victor slinking down the back path towards the dunny.

'What the hell are doing, you lazy little bugger? I told you to get that kindling chopped so your mother can light the heater.'

Vic cringed as the tears welled.

'I don't care if you want to go to the lavatory. You can just hold on instead of always trying to get out of the jobs you've been given. And stop that pathetic snivelling before I give you a bloody hiding.'

The snivelling continued and the strap came out. It was a heavy leather belt that Walter no longer wore now he'd lost so much weight. It was handy on the back of the veranda door. The violent rage eventually subsided as Victor crawled sobbing and choking off the veranda. The criss-crossed welts oozed blood down his legs and puddled into his socks as he lay whimpering behind the wash house.

'Bloody sook. What sort of a son are you?' Wal's coughing had started up with all the exertion.

This was to be Victor's lot from now on. He was thrashed mercilessly for anything and everything. Mostly for just being. He remained skinny into adolescence and his ears retained their jug-like appearance. Maybe it was this lack of physical vigour that so enraged his father, whose own frailty increased as his lungs crackled and disintegrated. His son's puny appearance made Wal wonder about how this useless streak of humanity was ever going to make any sort of a go at the whole sorry saga called life.

1938: A man in the making

Wal kept coughing but stayed alive. They were better off than some. Wal always had work even when the Depression came and there were so many unemployed waiting in queues at the soup kitchens. There were no more children, which was a blessing. He wasn't too sure why that happened but was relieved all the same. The frequent coughing bouts wore him down and there'd already been a couple of bouts of pneumonia. He'd lost some work time but nothing too serious and the Railways looked after their lot pretty well.

Victor had started at the workshop now and Walter thanked his lucky stars that he had got the apprenticeship. Actually, he seemed to be quite good at numbers. He still didn't have any bulk about him. Narrow little shoulders like a girl, Walter thought. But at least he wasn't completely useless. They caught the same train to and from work but travelled in different carriages. Victor still snivelled constantly. Must have been something wrong with his passages. It drove Walter mad.

He certainly couldn't have tolerated a twenty minute train journey listening to it. The pair were wary and kept out of each other's way as much as possible. The beatings had almost fizzled out. Wal just didn't have the stamina any more.

As Walter's lungs filled with muck more and more often, the doctor had to be consulted regularly. This learned man even reckoned the smoking was making Wal's chest worse but that didn't seem to make any sense.

One summer evening, his old army mate Bill dropped by to collect the spare bike tube he'd lent Walter. They were sitting on the back step enjoying a fag as Victor slunk past his father on his way to the outhouse. Walter's big head, framed by two quite prominent ears, was silhouetted against the back door.

'Jeez. He's the spitting image of you, Walter. A real chip off the old block.'

'Can't see the likeness myself. He's nothing like me. Must take after his mother.'

They each drag on their smokes and squint through the haze to a future neither chooses to imagine. They are ordinary blokes not given much to reflection. No good pontificating about what might or might not happen tomorrow or the next day.

Although there are odd occasions when Walter does brood briefly over Victor's future. Christ knows what kind of a man he could ever amount to.

Ballerinas

'A range of compulsive behaviours were described in
evidence. Behaviours included compulsive cleaning,
bed-making and general tidiness and obsessive hygiene
including showering and bathing and water use.'
Forgotten Australians

She mostly stays indoors with a carer now. But, for a few hours each day, she is unsupervised. The first of these unfettered hours she spends scrubbing her hands until blood seeps out of the cracked, inflamed skin. This leakage puzzles her as she pulls on rubber gloves to obscure the troubling spectacle. Then she pushes the wicker pram out of the double garage and sets off for the park. When her husband returns from work, he leads her gently home. The neighbours worried at first and reported her to various authorities. But eventually it was decided that she seemed safe enough. No one bothers her any more as she searches through rubbish bins looking for…something.

As she trudges through the dappled shade and the haze of not-knowing, the wheels of the old pram wheeze slightly, returning her to a time when the wheels of another pram squeaked into her consciousness. It is a memory from long, long ago.

A warm-smelling woman who is her mother holds her hand as they clamber onto a bus heading for the city to shop for weekly grocery supplies. By the time this exhausting mission is completed, her mother is weighed down with string bags bulging with tea, floor wax, flour, sugar, split peas and custard powder.

And it's time for a cup of tea.

Ahern's department store serves tea in bone china and Wendy-

Ann's mum is revived, even buoyed, by the tea and the sophisticated surroundings. Her mum admires good manners and correct protocol and seems at peace as Wendy-Ann guzzles her strawberry milkshake from a tall, tin cup. Back at the bus stop, time dawdles and Wendy-Ann feels sleepy. Her eyes are drooping when she catches a glimpse of…a witch.

Pushing an old pram with a torn hood and rusty wheels. Her face dark and craggy with a nose like a parsnip. Warts with hairs poking out are dotted on her chin and piled on her head are many hats. Felt hats with feathers and flowers crushed out of shape. Underneath the hats is a mountain of knots and frays like the stuffing out of a mattress. The colour of drain water. Cardigans and coats form layers of grey, black and brown. Between the jagged hems and the battered slippers are legs encased in thick woollen stockings hanging like curtains around her ankles. She stops at the bin and rummages. A few crushed packets are added to the pile of junk exploding from the pram. She walks past muttering to herself, staring into her pram.

Wendy-Ann hides behind her mum's skirt but is reassured at last that it's not really a witch. Just a lonely old lady who has lost her mind.

Wendy-Ann left the home in 1967 and began work as a cleaner in a regional pub. If there was one thing she was sure about, it was cleaning. Scrubbing, polishing, sweeping, dusting, washing, starching, ironing: all were stamped into her and she found both comfort and pride in attention to detail. Bed sheets and covers as smooth and white as a wedding cake were precisely aligned, mirrors dazzled, toilet porcelain sparkled, wooden floors reflected the legs of those passing over them. Behind this endowment, she grew confident enough to peek at the world, and when the manager complimented her work ethic, she blushed and lowered the dark eyelashes framing rather beautiful eyes. He fell for it and they were married eighteen months later. Robert also worked hard and was financially astute. Hence, they were able to settle into a comfortable home as soon as they married.

Rob was kind and generous. She was grateful and slightly amazed. Scared that it was all too good to be true and might just vanish like spirals of cigarette smoke. She became a bubbly young woman but underneath the grooming and sparkle she felt that she was play-acting. She felt guilty and ashamed that someone might discover her past, her pretence at normality. She was very particular about her appearance. Not necessarily in a vain way. It was more a compulsion. Keeping things, including herself, spotlessly clean and in order was paramount. It helped manage her world and was a measure of her worth. Robert appreciated his well-presented wife and neat home. He had moved into real estate after the hotel managing. He'd done well. There was a car and lots of attractive possessions.

Then she had fallen pregnant. A dream come true. A dream that morphed into a nightmare.

'You'll get over it and if your milk comes in, we'll take it for the premature babies,' said the briskly efficient midwife.

Her dead son had been bundled out of the delivery room wrapped in a way that looked just like a discarded packet of fish and chips. Dispatched to the incinerator along with other hospital waste. She never saw him. She never touched or smelled him. He was never named. There was no funeral. He just disappeared and nothing was ever mentioned.

After a week, she was sent home to 'get on with things'. She never talked about it and nor did anyone else, including her husband. There was a gaping abyss between them and neither knew how to bridge it. For so long she existed in a whirlpool of relentless grief. Her only child lost during that last hour. The beginning and end of a new life. Her body had not obliged and she had never conceived again. Rob buried his grief finally and became obsessed with making more money. It filled most of his hours and golf filled the rest. She filled her hours and her home with things. Lovely things that she would never have dreamed she could own all those years ago.

In those solitary hours allocated to the wife of a successful man, she cleaned, rearranged her beautiful things and swallowed the Valium tablets her doctor had prescribed for the perpetual sadness that clung to her. Through this fog of chemically dampened melancholy, she remained an exemplary housewife. But the years and the Valium had worn her down and she didn't feel any closer to God despite her clean things. The nightmares which snatched her from the depths of sleep grew more frequent. Her mind overflowed with voices and cries. Not her baby's cries, because his lungs had never filled. The cries seemed to come from a place further away. A glimpse of yellow net sometimes flashed into this far away world. Snapping sounds banished the sunny colour. A suitcase closing. A door banging and her mum's voice reminding her to be a good girl.

'It's just for a little while until Daddy gets better,' the voice reassured her.

She had never been told whether her daddy got better. Matron had quashed any enquiries about when her mum and dad were coming to get her.

'If your mother and father wanted you, they would have come to get you by now. Just be grateful that you have a roof over your head, young lady.'

She had learnt much later in life that her father had in fact died. A gambler, he was always close to the big win which would have transformed him into a dazzling knight sweeping his little family away from the dingy boarding house to a new brick and tile three by one in the suburbs. Instead, his legacy was debt. Her mum had moved to a country town where she could get work as a domestic for a well-to-do family. Distance and poverty were insurmountable obstacles. She never visited Wendy-Ann. There were letters. None of them were delivered. When Wendy-Ann left the home, she'd travelled by bus to the country town but her mum had moved on. No one had an address.

Over the years, her world grew more fuzzy as she groped her way through each day. Shards of her childhood jangled within her. Blurred faces from dormitories, bathrooms, laundries, dining halls, classrooms peered into her eyes. Smells of urine, vomit and cabbage crept into her nostrils. Sounds of screaming and yelling and sobbing played on and on. She cringed if someone moved too suddenly when she was waiting at the supermarket checkout. Moments of panic stopped her dead in her tracks in the shopping mall.

Yet, woven through these moments of terror were snatches of laughter and colour. Scenes of play with some other six-year-old kids. Not real play, just making up games whenever they could. Rubbing rags in circles, all in a row on hands and knees moving across a big wooden floor. Round and round until spots jumped in front of their eyes. A brief reprieve when Matron went out of the room and they became ballerinas, with the rags tied to their feet. Before her mind left her forever, Wendy-Ann had wondered if the ballet was her idea. Flashes of fuzzy yellow returned as she recalled a girl dressed as a fluffy duck. The girl was her. Her mummy and daddy were clapping as she bowed with all the other fluffy ducks. The memory invited a tiny upturning of her mouth until it was wiped away by the sounds of wailing as Matron returned and took the strap to them all.

Rob was concerned. He could see her drifting into a distant world. He cut back on golf.

'Why don't you come with me next week? I'm going over to Camden just out of Sydney to look at some property. It might be an enjoyable break for you,' he suggested.

She had agreed but already felt as exhausted and dislocated as the landscape in the small country town she was presently visiting. The streets linking the few hundred shabby houses were potholed with head-high weeds on each side. The houses were a mishmash of weatherboard, corrugated iron and pink brick cladding. Wire fences closeted snarling dogs of no obvious pedigree and the backyards and adjoining paddocks wore an unkempt cloak. Those with a tidy mind like hers found it unpalatable, reminiscent of homeless people in the city who wandered the streets clad in shreds of clothing and humanity. Rusty springs erupted from weeds telling of a past when beds were simple structures consisting of a horsehair mattress slung over a saggy spring base. Relics from a more orderly past consisted of leaning fence posts leering like ancient teeth half-heartedly containing a few bedraggled horses and goats that had lost interest in freedom. It all looked so sad that she wanted to be home within the ordered environment she had created. She disliked wide open spaces particularly those which offered no escape from wind, dirt, ravaging sun and disgusting insects. She wondered why she had agreed to come to this grubby backwater in the first place.

She swallowed more pills to counter the gnawing emptiness and continued walking. Amongst the debris she noticed something white. After scrambling through overgrown wild oats, she realised it was a pram. An old fashioned wicker pram just like the one she'd bought in the antique shop all those years ago, lovingly restoring it to its original splendour. A half covered rose bush tore at her new navy tights. The pain barely registered as a bloody trail trickled into her ankle boot.

It was quite a different pain which overwhelmed. It undid her. She was found roaming, nude and chanting in a tongue no one could decipher. Back home, she was sedated and hospitalised. Many months later, she went home but no one, including her husband, had any recollection of this person. Nor she of them.

The unkempt woman with the pram lurches on. Her eyes stare ahead and she continues the muttered conversation she is having with herself. A jogger stops to inquire as to whether she needs assistance. The young woman's attempts are without success and when she smiles into the pram she is shocked by what she sees. No gurgling baby. Just piles of dirty rags, plastic bags, old shoes, empty boxes, rotting fruit, greasy paper plates. And a stench rising in shimmering waves.

The jogger remains motionless as she watches. This woman whose face is vacant. Whose gait is uneven. Whose gaze is fixed. This woman who keeps moving neither seeing nor hearing. This woman with no edges. Searching…for something.

The Melting Tree

'The outcomes of serious abuse, assaults and deprivation suffered
by care leavers has had a complex, serious and negative impact
on their lives. At the most extreme, care leavers have lived a
half-life tainted by alienation, isolation and degradation.'
Forgotten Australians

At times, they share the melting branches with dozens of creaking cockatoos. Today, however, Georgie, her sister and brother have it to themselves and are arranged at varying heights according to age. Her sister is the highest; Georgie feels quite brave two metres off the ground and their brother is hidden somewhere between the two.

This giant remnant from settler days holds its secrets as firmly as it holds the ground beneath its polished leather leaves. Its aerial roots have fallen from branches for nearly two centuries, buttressing the massive canopy. Hidden from view is a system of subterranean roots whose tangled web creeps silently into territory far from the trunk. A surreal sculpture, this living organism connects different realms: the real, the imagined and the spaces between.

From their elevated platform they hear Billy's back door bang shut. He must have finished watering his tomato plants. The kids scramble down, grab their bikes and head for home.

'Where have you been? It's nearly dinner time.' Their mother has had a long day. The thinness of her voice reminds them of this. 'Remember to put those bikes away properly. Well? Where have you been all this time?'

Her sister and brother barge past Georgie in their rush to get through the door first. Sometimes she wishes she were the oldest. But she is only six and still pretty wobbly on her bike. Which is why she is always last home. She trips in her rush to dump the pink two-wheeler on the pile outside the back door.

It's her sister who responds to their mother's fractious enquiries. Her voice is thick with the importance of information. 'Down near old Billy's place.'

'Who is Billy?'

'He lives down the next street. The house near the melting tree.'

'What on earth are you talking about? A melting tree?'

'The branches are all melted down to the ground. Like it's made of goo.'

Their mother scoffs at such an idea.

Georgie's sister continues to inform. 'Sometimes we sit on his veranda. He's got a jar of lollies for kids.'

Their mother's lips are a piece of string as she absorbs this news. 'I don't think you should be on his veranda. And I certainly don't think accepting lollies from a stranger is appropriate.'

'Aw, Mum. That's not fair. Billy's not even a stranger. He just likes to talk to kids sometimes.'

The subject is closed as they are pointed towards the bathroom.

They trudge off whinging and shoving. A fight over who pushes the soap dispenser erupts before they finally troop back and settle on the bar stools. Their mother serves their meal.

'I don't like fat spaghetti,' whines Georgie.

The Moreton Bay fig was planted outside the first schoolhouse sometime in the 1830s. It has shaded kids for generations and served as a lookout for the community. You could spot a bush fire or peer into backyards from its grey-brown branches. Its trunk, smoothed by time, has invited adventurers and tempted the imaginative to dream. And for those less courageous it has provided a cool place of reflection. Underground, silent tendrils have connected different lives and this web now embraces the house where Georgie lives, the mysterious swamp where Georgie dreams, and Billy's old weatherboard house where Georgie chats as she munches on forbidden lollies. There is a tangle of fibres creeping under Georgie's back fence, although Steve and Alice know nothing of the fig roots linking them to Billy and the swamp.

Once the children are settled for the night, Alice raises the subject which has been worrying her since dinner time.

'Did I tell you that the kids were hanging around that old fellow Billy's place today?'

'Not that odd bloke who lives by himself in the old settler's cottage?'

'Yes. The house near the Moreton Bay fig tree.'

'Well, I suppose he seems harmless enough, but I'm not sure he's quite right in the head.'

'Harmless or not, he's been giving them lollies, which I find quite disturbing. I've told them to keep away.'

Billy sips his cup of tea in the shade of the vast fig tree. Its branches extend over most of his yard sparing one sunny patch where he grows a few vegies. He loves the majestic tree and often shares his thoughts with this comforting living relic. He finds faces in the gnarly forms on the trunk and chats to them. No one, except little Georgie, listens so patiently. The tree soaks up Billy's secrets along with the moisture it stealthily garners from Billy's vegie garden.

He exists quietly and simply enough by himself and enjoys chatting to passing children happily sharing his jar of lollies, even his favourite humbugs. Lollies are his only extravagance. The rest of his pension is carefully allocated for his living expenses by his sister Janet, who visits once a month. He likes living in a house by himself much better than sharing with other needy people. The group-care houses he's lived in before were busy all the time. The carers were always making him do things and sometimes he liked just doing nothing. When Janet had finally tracked him down, he was already in his fifties. He couldn't remember her very clearly. She was five and he was eight when they'd been sent to different homes.

'You like it here, don't you, Billy? Do you talk to people sometimes?'

Janet speaks to his right side. He's deaf in the left ear from the repeated bashings. How much other damage his already under-wired brain had suffered would never be known.

'Just the kids. Like Georgie. They play in the tree next door.'

'Well, that's good, Billy. I'm glad.'

Georgie is his favourite visitor. She sits next to him on his old sofa and talks to him as though he were normal. She never laughs when he doesn't know the answer to things like why don't silk worms eat lettuce leaves? Or why do cats have nine lives? It doesn't matter to Georgie. She is happy to just wonder with Billy.

There are some kids who ride their bikes past his house and call him names. 'What are ya, Billy? A spazzo or what?' as they skid their wheels in front of his yard and lob spit on his driveway.

They poke their tongues at him and are definitely not nice children. A few other little kids stop sometimes to get a lolly from his jar. He likes them but not the tongue-pokers and spitters.

It's that time of the month and Janet has called in to check up on things. 'Has your little friend Georgie been to visit lately?'

'Nup. She must have forgot.'

Billy is used to his own company. He's used to watching from the edges.

A Moreton Bay fig is also known as a strangler fig. It germinates in the top of another tree and as it enlarges it gradually strangles its host. It may grow to fifty metres, with a canopy spread over the same distance. What is underground replicates the dimensions above. The roots of the melting tree crept into the swamp long ago. They tangle through and around the foundations of the paperbarks and into the sludgy water.

Since their mother's prohibitions, the three children have kept off Billy's veranda and are now engrossed in more exciting adventures around the stinking swamp. Once the overgrown track has been conquered, kids from all around are joining in the boggy explorations. High grass and water reeds create a dense jungle setting with unexpected stuff lurking in hidden places. Half buried in the murk they're discovering old bits of bikes and shopping trolleys. Each foray has revealed a new discovery. Some are seriously spooky. Like the skull of an animal with huge teeth grinning at them.

'It's a cow,' decided Jimmy, who was the oldest.

''Tis not. Cows don't have those kind of teeth,' challenged Claire, who was going to be a vet.

'Well, what is it then, smarty pants?'

'I reckon it's a horse,' she proclaimed with some confidence. She went horse riding once a week and was advanced enough to put the bridle on herself. The stubborn mouth which refused to open for her was barred by such teeth.

It's finally agreed that it must be a horse when further muddy relics turn out to be a couple of horseshoes.

Georgie watches wide-eyed during this episode. She loves horses and is amazed at the weird skull with its massive gaping eye sockets and those leering teeth. Where was the velvety muzzle she fondled when she fed carrots to the horse that grazed in the paddock near the school? And what about the beautiful soft eyes that gazed lovingly at her as she rummaged for the treats in her bag? This bony structure didn't seem to have any relationship to that wondrous creature. Georgie dreams of having her own horse. It would be glossy and black and she would keep it in the backyard, where she would ride it round and round. With her long hair billowing behind, she would gallop and gallop. Her fingers would twist in the black mane as they were transported to a world where she would ride horses and eat ice cream all day. And she would be the oldest not the youngest in the family.

She returns from her reverie to the swamp, where the explorers have turned up an old television set with the screen smashed in and a microwave with the door hanging by one hinge. They start setting up their finds on a patch of raised ground. They name it the Spooky

Castle. Offcuts of four by two timber serve as a narrow and suitably precarious bridge across the murky moat.

The weeks march on and it is always a race to see who can get away from home first and resume residence at the Spooky Castle. The most senior members squabble for the position on the throne fashioned out of a battered shopping trolley with no wheels. But, if you're there first, even a junior member can bask in the power of an elevated view of the swampy estate. Until your seat is usurped by the next older kid who turns up. Of the tribe of swamp dwellers, Georgie is also the youngest.

Back at Georgie's house, Steve brings up the subject of Billy again. 'Are the kids keeping away from that old bloke? All these reports about paedophilia worry me.'

'They've been busy making cubbies down near the swamp, so they seem to have forgotten about him.'

Steve is thoughtful. 'I know how the media can drum up paranoia and it may well be that Billy is just a lonely old man. But you can never be sure about some people.'

Moreton Bay figs can be destructive. Their roots can damage piping, invade sewerage systems, undermine foundations of buildings and vandalise the smooth surfaces of paving and roadways. Alternatively, these trees and their cousins can be a symbol of eternal life. The seemingly unending capacity for the roots to expand under the earth's surface gives rise to this mythology. And perhaps the roots also transmit secrets along their knotty fibres.

Something has alerted Georgie to a new possibility at the Spooky Castle on this Saturday morning. All the other kids are busy. Sporting events and shopping excursions have filled their timetables. Today she has no events and is at home by herself. Well, almost. Her mum is in the backyard mulching the vegetable garden and listening to relaxing music through her headphones. The idea of occupying the shopping trolley throne without any big kids is compelling and Georgie is drawn down the street and onto the hidden track.

It's some time before her mum realises that she's not in the house. She dials Steve's number. 'Is Georgie with you?'

Steve reassures her. 'I'm sure she's not far away. I'll be home in ten minutes.'

They're not panicking yet as they ring friends and drive up and down the local streets.

'She never goes off by herself,' Alice keeps saying. 'She knows not to do that.'

Georgie rubs her hand over the tree's weird lumps and bulges as she passes on her way to the track. The branches creak and the cockatoos rasp. There is no sign of any other life as she crosses the drawbridge and clambers onto the rickety, regal structure. There aren't too many rules in her household but Georgie knows that she isn't to leave the yard without her older siblings. She won't be too long and her mum probably won't even miss her.

Or she'll really cop it when she gets home but it's worth it. There's no one to boss her around. She surveys her realm with a sense of enormous satisfaction. Sunlight bounces off the water between the reeds, creating an illusion of transparency, which in reality doesn't exist. On closer inspection, the oily, sluggish liquid bears little resemblance to water, yet in this light it becomes an ornamental lake on which white swans may settle at any moment. Framing her magic world are the twisted configurations of paperbarks, probably inhabited by elves and fairies, which she much prefers to the horrid banksia men she's seen in Gran's old picture book.

She confers with her doll Bette about how they might catch a swan and ride on its back. 'We can make reins out of reeds, and it would be even better than riding a horse because we can fly in the sky,' whispers Georgie.

In the recesses of her mind, there is a growing suspicion that fairies and swans carrying children don't really exist. However, she isn't quite ready to dismiss them from her imaginary world.

The cockies continue to squeak and saw as the sun climbs higher. Georgie's throne is still cool in the shadow of the vast, leafy umbrella. The birds have settled and tree remains silent and timeless. Time for Georgie also stands still. How long she has occupied this magic realm is unclear. When she hears sounds, alerting her to imposters, she casts around for a place to hide. The melting tree seems her only option but sneaking along the track to its base is hazardous. What if she meets the intruders on the track? She'll be found out. She decides instead to wade through the swampy water. She can bypass most of the track that way and the tall reeds will hide her from view. Then she can climb the tree and look down on whoever it is spoiling her glorious day.

She clutches Bette to her chest as she cautiously steps into the sludge. She is surprised by how cold it is. And how deep. The mushy bottom seems to go down and down. Tangles of weed and broken sticks grab at her.

It's the roots of the fig tree which finally hold her securely.

The police and volunteers search throughout the day. There is no sign of a little girl wearing a Dorothy Dinosaur T-shirt and orange shorts. Blonde with blue eyes. Aged six. They visit the home of the old bloke Billy. Twice, just to be sure. He is quite teary because he really likes little Georgie. They search backyards, inside garden sheds, under culverts, the empty school grounds, the surrounding scrub and around the Moreton Bay fig. They scan the area around the swamp but there is nothing to indicate that a little girl has been a queen on a throne. There is just an old shopping trolley and some abandoned junk. Water police are on their way. They will use divers to trawl through the water.

Just before dusk, they find her. Slimy and lifeless, her small body is zipped into a bag.

While a family which once numbered five but is now only four packs up and wordlessly leaves town, Billy remains on the edges. No one takes much notice of this strange and silent man. The lolly jar is no longer on the veranda and when he is not sharing life's mysteries with the faces on the Melting Tree, he spends time sitting on a log near the Spooky Castle. It's quiet now the kids have left. They've been forbidden by overwrought parents and their own bravado has evaporated. Even the Melting Tree is out of bounds, inhabited only by the roosting cockatoos settling like old floor joists into the night. Its roots continue their journey towards new places and new stories.

After a week or so, a doll floats to the surface of the turgid water. Old Billy finds it and sits it on his sideboard. The head lolls at an odd angle and the hair streaked with dried-out slime only partially covers the pink plastic scalp. The eyes no longer open and close. Although she stares without blinking, the doll listens patiently.

An Ordinary Woman

A young lady

The face, reflected in the window of the trolley bus, is smudged with grubby finger marks. But even through these smears it is clear that it is a face in the process of collapse. Behind the functionally framed Coke-bottle lenses, the eyes belonging to this face are awash and the pudgy, slightly spotty cheeks are sodden. The owner of this wretched visage is no longer Number 24. She is a 'young lady' with a real name. Janet Marshall. Knowledge of this transformation was delivered yesterday by Matron.

'Well, young lady. Your stay here is over. Here is a letter of introduction to the manager of the Leederville Laundry. You will be dropped off at the bus terminus at eight a.m. That will be all. Close the door after you.'

Bewildered by this abrupt alteration to the shape of her life, Janet had scrambled up the steps of the number 6 trolley bus clutching the battered cardboard case that contained both a relic from her past and the necessities for her future. A cotton brassiere and two pairs of cotton panties. Brown socks, green cotton pyjamas, one navy serge skirt, one white blouse, one navy woollen cardigan, a sanitary belt, two sanitary pads, a toothbrush, a comb and a tin of pristine Lakeland coloured pencils, the latter a gift from her father from so long ago. She's kept them tucked under her mattress for the intervening thirteen years. Just before leaving the institution that had been her home, she had slipped them into her suitcase. Now with the case jammed between her dimply knees, the shock of her expulsion into an unknown world overwhelms.

Eventually, the silent sobbing subsides. The envelope gripped in her clammy hands has come unstuck. She peeps inside, afraid of admonishment. There is none. She is quite alone. There are no voices barking instructions or insults. No cruel hands delivering blows. Nothing. Just the whirr of the bus as it follows the overhead wires through the streets to her destination. Leederville Commercial Laundry, 16 Oxford Street, Leederville.

Another glimpse inside the envelope reveals the folded introductory letter, a two-dollar note and a creased slip of paper. Janet gingerly removes the slip and opens it out.

BIRTH IN THE STATE OF WESTERN AUSTRALIA				
ILD	PARENTS	INFORMANT	WITNESS	REGISTRAR
th May 1949	Father Robert James Marshall 29 years Painter	Certified in writing by Robert James Marshall	Dr H.L. Cook	G.R. Hathway
net Elizabeth	Mother Mary Susan Brambles 29 years		A.M. Walsh	24th May 1949
male	Married 28th September 1945	Residence 44 Tate Street, West Leederville	S. Cummings	Perth

Time is frozen as Janet battles to decipher the writing. She's spent most of her childhood in the laundry, so her reading skills are limited and she has never progressed to the nibs and inkwells required for mastering the flourishing script of this document. Yet eventually she recognises this scrap of paper as what must be the record of her birth. Proof of her very existence. Janet Elizabeth Marshall. She didn't even know she had a middle name. And proof of a real mother and father. Robert James and Mary Susan. Her birth date swims back into focus. There have been no birthdays all these years in the home. No gifts, no cakes, no candles.

She shakily returns the slip to the envelope and stares out through the grime into an alien universe.

Stranded on the concrete pathway, Janet also becomes rock. Her senses petrified. There are no sounds or smells or textures. She has found the wrought-iron gate with a number five painted on the curlicue frame. It matches the number scribbled on a scrap of paper by Mr Green, the manager of the laundry.

'The landlady is Mrs Kent,' he said. 'She runs a suitable boarding house for young ladies.'

Her glasses are coated with dried tears and greasy blotches, so the world around her is a blurry fog as she stands and stands, willing the return of her imaginary world and her sweet-smelling mummy. A special and secret place only she can enter. But through the haze, Janet senses movement; at the end of the path, the front door opens and a tiny woman in a mauve dress walks towards her. At least that's what Janet thinks she can see. It is when this silhouette speaks that Janet's vision begins to clear and she can hear again.

'Hello, Janet. How lovely to meet you. I've been expecting you.'

The pastel shape, who is Mrs Kent, smiles, lifts up the suitcase, gently takes Janet's hand and leads her into her new home. With her own room. With a pink bed cover. With a cake of lavender soap sitting on the pillow. With a chocolate wrapped in shiny paper as a little present. Because today is Janet's birthday.

'Mr Green telephoned me about a room and he noticed your birth date when he opened the envelope. Happy birthday, Janet. I'll make a special sponge cake to celebrate at teatime.'

Soft arms embrace. Mrs Kent is a woman whose shape and smell is that of a mother despite never having had children of her own. The taut wires fastening Janet together begin to loosen.

This smiling woman doesn't have wings or a wand, but it is the beginning of something magic. From this moment, Mrs K (that's what she's affectionately called by her young ladies) believes in Janet until Janet begins to believe in herself. It is Mrs K who nurtures and loves, as Janet reconstructs broken bits of herself and goes bravely to work each morning at the Leederville Commercial Laundry.

Janet's bedroom door has a key. She locks her door and sits on her bed when she gets home from work. It's so quiet after the racket of the laundry. Mrs K is in the kitchen making tea and the other three boarders aren't home yet. She opens the secret door to her eggshell-blue world and talks to her mum. She tells her about work and about Mrs K. There are other things she tells her sometimes.

'Men aren't allowed in our boarding house, Mummy. But I still get scared at night. I have nightmares. About Mr White. Grunting. The stink of sweat – and grog – and cigarettes. Sometimes I wake up crying. I have to keep my eyes squeezed shut to block out his flabby guts and brown teeth. I wish you were here, Mummy. Mrs White called me a dirty, filthy creature. I was so frightened when they sent me back to the home. No one said anything. Then the doctor pushed his long green gloves inside me and made me scream. I was only ten.'

Janet stares and stares at a spot on her bedroom wall and wonders what her mum and dad would look like now. She can hardly remember their faces. She was only five when she went to the home. No one had told her why she had to stay there. Or where Susie and Billy had gone.

'I didn't know that you never got better, Mummy. I can still remember the time when I had to go to Matron's office. She told me to sit down. Her voice was always crabby so when she started to talk in a soft voice, I knew something was wrong straight away. Then she said that Daddy was dead. He'd been killed in an accident. She said she was sorry and that it was a tragedy. I remember that my mind and the vase of flowers on Matron's desk started to spin and make patterns in my head. Through the swirling colours my voice was very far away when I asked Matron where you were. She just told me not to be so silly. You were dead too. That's why I came to the home. Then she told me to go back to my work and to shut the door behind me.'

Back in her bedroom, the alarm clock ticks loudly. It's new – or nearly new. It's the first thing that Janet has ever bought. She found it in the Good Samaritan shop near her work. Before washing her face and hands for tea, Janet tells her mum about the young man at work who has been kind to her.

'His name is Reg. We sit on the lunch bench together. He's shy like me but he smiles at me, which is more than anyone else ever does. They're all stuck-up and think home kids are no good. He has jam sandwiches mainly but Mrs Kent makes me polony and tomato sauce most days. It's my favourite and Reg told me that it's his favourite as well. Yesterday we talked a bit more and I swapped my polony for his jam sandwich. I like Reg. He doesn't make me feel stupid. Or dirty. Or ugly.'

A friend

Reg and Janet are eating their sandwiches. Janet finds the familiarity of their brief and predictable communications comforting. There is a pattern to their daily exchange.

Until one lunchtime when he bends towards her and whispers, 'Someone told me that you're a homie. Are you really?'

The wooden bench under Janet's broad bottom turns to water and the world around her becomes soggy tissue paper. The sounds and smells in the lunch room vanish and her imaginary blue world comes hurtling back. The minutes bounce off the walls as Janet's body remembers. She dashes to the bathroom and bits of polony and tomato sauce and white bread splash up the porcelain.

Locked inside the toilet cubicle, she whispers to her mum through the snot and tears. 'I thought that Reg was a good person but maybe I can't tell what kind people are really like. Some people said that Matron was a kind person, but they didn't see her belting the daylights out of those two girls who tried to run away. They didn't hear the screams as she shoved them under the stairs and left them in the dark all night. And when they came back to the dormitory, they just kept crying… and crying…and crying. Even when their bruises faded and their cuts healed, they said they were always scared and had broken bits banging inside their heads.'

The lunch siren goes and Janet splashes her face in the basin, rubs her glasses on the hem of her uniform and sneaks back to the ironing room. The afternoon unfolds around a girl who is nothing more than a terrified, dumb home kid.

She tells Mrs K that she's not well and doesn't have any tea. Mrs K brings her a tray with a cup of tea and hot buttered toast. Janet sobs herself to sleep.

It takes all her courage to return to the laundry next morning, urged on by the voice playing in her head. Her mother's soothing voice telling her that she is really a good girl and that she loves her. A voice that reassures her that there are other nice people just like Mrs K and that she shouldn't listen to the voices of nasty people from the past hissing that she is just a dirty little girl who smells of wee. Who tell her that her mother and father never loved her. That no one would ever love her because she doesn't deserve to be loved. Who hit her when she cries and can't eat her cold porridge. Who shout as they hit her again and make her eat the vomit lumps sprayed all over the plate. Who snap and snarl as their eyes bore holes through her. Who twist her arms and ears to make her listen. Her mother's comforting voice keeps telling her to forget about those people but Janet's mind keeps remembering.

Reg is waiting on the lunch bench for her. She stares at the brown, lino floor so she doesn't have to look at him.

Reg leans towards her and whispers, 'I'm a homie too.'

Janet stops chewing and holds her breath. Eventually she darts a sideways glance at him. He is smiling at her. Not just with his mouth. His eyes look kind and they're smiling too.

So he tells her about the home that he went to when he was four. He supposes that his mum and dad are dead and he doesn't know if he has any brothers or sisters. Janet keeps munching her sandwich while Reg remembers the beatings and the other awful stuff that he thought would kill him. He doesn't remember any kind people. But he didn't die, so now he's going to make a go of things. He's saving up to buy a car.

The smiles exchanged between them become more regular.

A fiancée

It is more than a year since Janet started at the laundry.

Reg is her friend but it's still a shock when he says, 'Why don't we go for a picnic at Kings Park on Sunday?'

The sky is streaked with fairy floss clouds as she waits for Reg at the bus stop. Her best dress mirrors the patches of blue above her and her seamless stockings slip smoothly into the white slingback shoes. She looks lovely according to Mrs K. Reg is on time and he's wearing brown trousers and a checked shirt. He looks very smart. They smile hesitantly and board the bus.

They both have the jitters and don't have much to say as they find a spot near the pond and settle on the tartan rug that his landlady has lent him. Mrs Kent has slipped two pieces of her jam sponge cake into a paper bag along with the sandwiches. Ham and gherkin. Something a bit special, Mrs K had said. Reg has a thermos of tea. They watch the ducks squabble over the sandwich crusts and laugh.

Going home, a face peers at Janet from the smeary bus window. It's the face of an ordinary young lady whose spots have subsided and whose eyes and mouth are smiling.

The picnic outings become a pattern. Perhaps once a month, the two timid friends grow used to one another as they sit on a tartan rug overlooking a majestic river. There is laughter. A dog runs off with a man's hat. Ducks sneak scraps from the woollen rectangle that is their shared world. Unexpected showers of rain make them run for shelter shrieking like children. The always cordial and gentle partings as they leave each other at the bus stop.

This routine is safe. There are no unexpected occurrences. The same bus stop, the same destination, the same sandwiches, the same tartan rug.

Until Reg dares to suggest something different and Janet's chest stands still. In trepidation.

'Why don't we go to the Saturday afternoon pictures?' he ventures.

The bus stop remains the same. And the destination proves a success as Janet and Reg grow accustomed to this new adventure.

At interval, the theatre becomes a circus as kids pelt each other with Jaffas. Reg buys two ice creams in cardboard buckets each with a little wooden spoon. They sit in the same seats and have a good laugh at Tom and Jerry and scream along with all the kids as Tarzan swings from branches in the jungle. Their hands remain in their own laps.

Yet they both seem to sense a tenuous love as fragile as eggshells. They are so careful with each other. They cradle this precious thing and never interrogate. They glance and smile often, each reassuring the other that this blossoming is real.

The faces reflected side by side in the bus window are at peace. Hands, resting on the seat, brush against each other as the bus lurches. Neither recoils. Over many journeys, these hands, once sticky and sweaty, mould to one another, becoming soft and warm. Touching becomes safe. Slowly, wounds of the spirit and soul are sealed. Reg and Janet are quiet people. They experiment with kindness. It suits them. They learn together about respect, about trust. They lock away the memories of neglect, of cruelty, of abuse. In each other they find a good person. They hold hands at the pictures like ordinary people.

Another year passes with outings to the park and the pictures. Added to the repertoire are Saturday-night pictures where all-time favourites are screened. Sometimes they see the same film over and over. Tonight they're watching Janet's favourite, *My Fair Lady*, for the third time. She loves Audrey Hepburn and imagines learning to talk just like her. At the end they stand up with everyone to sing 'God Save the Queen'. The Queen, as always, looks beautiful astride her horse, smiling out at her subjects.

Going home on the bus, their hands are cemented together. Reg walks her to her gate and gives her a little peck on the cheek. Janet's glasses and their noses are obstacles and their lips don't touch. She feels embarrassed but goes off to bed with a warm fuzzy feeling.

The velvet seats and smoky darkness sooth. Janet and Reg love the intimate space and vicarious thrills. *West Side Story* dazzles with its music, dance and colour. The poignancy of its ending is not lost to either of them. They are both stunned when Tony is killed and he and Maria can never marry. It is their first viewing and Janet's face is streaming as the lights come up. Reg is swiping at his eyes with a handkerchief. On the way home in the bus, they don't say much.

Reg is holding Janet's hand tighter than usual. He squeezes it and whispers, 'Why don't we get married?'

Janet can't be sure of what she has heard. 'Us? Get married?'

Reg grips her hand and nods.

Janet's hand clutches hard. Her throat is parched but she finally finds the words. 'Yes. I would like that.'

Janet is a fiancée.

A bride

In the privacy of her pink bedroom, Janet continues her conversations with her mum. Tonight she pulls the suitcase from under her bed, carefully lifting out each item and arranging it on the chenille bedspread. She often shares this secret ritual with her mother. Her glory box. Janet has never imagined she would be the proud owner of such a receptacle. It reminds her that she is a real fiancée.

At first it was a shoebox but now everything is neatly packed into a suitcase, at the bottom of which is the box of Lakeland pencils, still with perfectly sharpened coloured points. The period of engagement has passed the twelve-month mark and Janet has been adding to the collection with her modest savings. Lots of little things for the house like pillowslips, tea towels, tablecloths and doilies.

'Do you like the lace edging on the doilies?' she asks her mum.

Janet's fingers stray as usual to the sensuous satin fabric of her bridal underwear. All matching: a cream satin underwire brassiere, panties and full petticoat. And all edged with cream lace. The pure white of the patent shoes, satin gloves and frothy veil dazzle as they lay on the pink bed. And the apricot, nylon nightdress with shoestring straps still evokes an intake of breath as Janet imagines herself gliding towards the marital bed.

'Mrs K is making my wedding dress,' she explains. 'Here's the material. It's crêpe. Mrs K said it would drape really well. The style is the Empire line.'

Janet gazes at the photo on the Simplicity dress pattern. The glamour of being a bride. She is still astonished that it is Janet Elizabeth Marshall who will become such a vision of splendour.

'I'm so lucky to have Mrs K to make my dress. And that isn't all. She said that she'll make a two-tiered wedding cake as well. With royal icing roses. And wedding figurines on the top. She is the kindest person I know. It's almost like having a real family. As though you and Daddy were here again.'

At present, the figurines for the wedding cake are waiting patiently on the top of the fridge. Janet is transfixed by their miniature perfection. The handsome smiling face of the groom and the delicate beauty of the bride with her rosebud lips. Lips that remind her of her doll Belinda. She still misses her childhood confidante and wonders if she's still in the playroom at the home. A room Janet was allowed to visit once when she was about eight. A room for important visitors to inspect. Her bruises had faded enough to be one of the chosen and, dressed in a pretty frock with shiny shoes and frilly socks, she had spied Belinda on a shelf too high to reach. Although the perfect rosebud lips still smiled at her just like the tiny ceramic bride's do now.

'It's hard to imagine that Reg and I will be just like those little figures. Sometimes they make me wonder about what you and Daddy must have looked like on your wedding day.'

Janet has no remnants of her childhood. No photos, no mementos. She is luckier than most. She has a birth certificate.

The pelting rain and blustery wind has been replaced by a still breezy but warm spring. Janet is standing in her cotton bra and half-slip with a podgy stomach bulging between the two. If she stops breathing, she can pull it in while Mrs K slips the partly completed dress over her head. Janet loves the pattern. A scooped neckline and flared elbow length sleeves. To her, the crêpe folds look like a waterfall splashing down from the bust line.

Mrs K tells her how much it suits her figure. 'You'll look ravishing on the big day,' she says.

Ravishing. No one has ever called her that before.

The dress is finished, with only the hem to be pinned. Janet wobbles as she stands on the kitchen table looking into the big mirror propped against the cupboards. She barely recognises herself. She is transformed from a chubby, plain girl with glasses to a princess whose life stretches ahead promising happiness ever after.

Her wedding day. The girls in the household are excited and Mrs K is in a fluster. The morning is perfect. Not a cloud in the bluest of blue skies. The butterflies in Janet's stomach refuse to settle even after two cups of strong tea and two slices of toast and marmalade. The other girls use the bathroom early so that it's available for her to luxuriate in a bath perfumed with special bath salts. She washes her hair and Mrs Kent sets it with big rollers then bundles her into the backyard. Clad in her pink flannel dressing gown and with a pile of *Women's Weeklies*, Janet plays at being a lady while her hair dries in the mild spring sunshine. For morning tea, Mrs Kent brings out a cup of Nescafé and a slice of her fabulous jam sponge.

'Here we are, my dear. Need to keep your strength up, don't we?' Mrs K also has her hair up in rollers and a net. And she is almost as excited as she had been on her own wedding day, she says.

'Thanks, Mrs K. You're really spoiling me today!'

'And so I should.'

Mrs K disappears through the fly wire while Janet floats. Looking down, she can see a figure in pink as the centrepiece in a red square.

Huge sausage shapes balance on the figure's head, flashing copper and gold under a white sky. Crimson balls beside her sway gently in a slight breeze and bright yellow and orange jewels dazzle as they move around on a grey carpet dotted with rocks of jade. An ordinary space transformed to a place over the rainbow. And the figure at its centre is her.

It is the chickens' squawking under the oleander bush that return her to the concrete square in a suburban yard with a bed of slightly wilted tomato plants beside her. Her happiness fills her to bursting.

Then fear nudges its way into her soul. What if she doesn't deserve Reg and Mrs Kent and a white wedding? What if it all just disappears like her mum and dad and sister and brother? Flashes of doubt snap at the edges of her mind. Would Reg know that she isn't a virgin? Would she have to return to that secret locked-away place deep inside her to explain the awfulness of Mr White? Her stomach churns as fragments of those memories disable her. She is frozen in the unravelling wicker chair. Smells and sounds and sensations from that little bedroom belonging to the kind couple who fostered her, render her eyes and ears useless to the real world. Shame bubbles from some deep part of her smothering her joy.

It takes Mrs Kent considerable effort to rouse Janet from this unexplained torpor, get her inside, splash her face with cold water and transform her into a radiant bride. Which she does, and Janet (without her glasses) looks more beautiful than she could ever have imagined. And Reg, resplendent in his hired penguin suit, agrees as he holds his breath and looks up the aisle. Janet can't actually see clearly who she is marrying but she is certain of the cloak of security and commitment this special person throws over her troubled soul. She feels lucky. She feels loved. She feels safe.

Minutes and hours and years merge into decades. Janet glances at the hall mirror as she passes. She sees a smiling, resilient and extraordinary woman.

Australia Fair

'This report is not just concerned with the past, it is very much
about the present and it informs the future of our nation.'
Forgotten Australians

At first, Amber experienced a sense of disbelief when she heard Bev's story. Later, she would recognise how these revelations changed her. But the sense that this dark history may replay itself with her as an actor was something she could never have predicted.

I just don't get it! How could all that shit possibly have happened without someone doing something about it?

Amber's face is puce with incredulity. It clashes terribly with her blue hair. The spiky bits are electric. So is the aura around her.

Kaz knows well enough not to challenge when she's in this mode. But he does show interest.

Yeah, well. I guess maybe no one knew too much in those days. There was no Facebook and stuff, remember.

It doesn't work.

Jesus, Kaz. I fucking totally understand that there was no social media. But this wasn't Dickens' fucking London I'm talking about. This was only about fifty years ago right here in Perth.

Well, I wasn't fucking there, was I? So how would I know about this shit?

There's only so much he can take of her outrage. He's studying engineering. Facts and figures soothe him. There are neat calculations, which come to satisfactory conclusions. The humanities leave him floundering. Everyone has an idea and no one tells you which one is right.

Anyway, I'm pissing off to the Olds' place. I'll hang out there for a while and chill out.

He has piles of dirty clothes and his mum always cooks great meals when he goes home. Amber's a good chick but he just needs time out.

Whatever.

She loads the juicer and flicks the switch. Any further discussion is obliterated by the screaming gadget churning out beetroot, kale, chia seeds and spinach.

Catch ya soon, babe.

Kaz gives her a hopeful grin then he's out the door with a green garbage bag full of his stuff. He might get a Macca's on the way.

Amber takes her tumbler of wholesome goodness back to the computer, where she dips into report after report about an issue that she's just beginning to uncover: stories about 'forgotten Australians'. First of all, Bev next door, then by chance she'd come across a collection of stories about the same thing. Systematic and endemic child abuse in institutional care. Like a sniffer dog, she is now hunting down historical sources. What she is finding takes her breath away. Disbelief, anger and overwhelming sadness surge through her whole being in alternating gushes. Like a river in flood, transporting flotsam and depositing debris along the banks, garbage gathers around her edges but her life goes on despite this unsettling new knowledge. Her shape is somehow altered and she is no longer able to unknow this disturbing past.

This weather is freezing her bum off. Her days and nights are filled with part-time work and uni assignments. Kaz hasn't come back. She's not sure whether that's good or bad. She misses the sex and a warm body in bed but maybe that's all. She's not really in the mood for his smelly socks and sci-fi movies any more. Kaz is kind of sweet but rather an empty vessel. He's functional and non-aggressive. He can be funny and he's good in bed. Good attributes, she recognises, but maybe she needs more. She's moved on, with an increasingly cringing response to the me, me, me focus of her peer group. Maybe, she thinks somewhat tentatively, this is the blossoming of maturity. Or is she just an uptight sex-starved bitch?

She begins unfriending some of her Facebook contacts. The constant bullshit about nail technicians and eyelash extensions is beginning to bore her senseless. God. Maybe worse, she's becoming a nerd. She can't get her mind off the stuff about kids in welfare organisations. Her once simple world view is skewed. The grid of meaning established during her safe and comfortable childhood has been dismantled. She's always known that kids in developing countries suffered abuse and neglect but she had been reared to believe that in ethical, wealthy countries like her own these practices, along with slavery, had been abandoned centuries ago. So how come the bullshit stories about how wonderful and democratic and fair everything was in good old Australia have never been shot down? She's mightily pissed off, to be honest. Like finding out there's no tooth fairy and that her tiny, pearly baby teeth have been chucked in the bin by her mum. Same kind of fairy story. Everyone believing that good, Christian souls looked after these kids when exactly the opposite was happening. They were beating the crap out of them.

How twisted and vicious do you have to be to ignore sick kids and just let them die? Or beat the daylights out of them for spilling a drink. Or make them eat their own vomit. Or rape them over and over again, she screams down the phone to her friend Storm.

Storm has never heard of the 'forgotten Australians'.

Fuck! That's just what I'm trying to tell you. No one seems to know about this stuff.

Fuck you too, Amber. You're so preachy and full of shit. You need to chill out.

But Amber is in no mood to chill out. Getting wasted has lost its appeal. And Storm is a fucking philistine. She's definitely going to unfriend her too.

The more she searches, the more she unearths the lying, the culture of silence, the justifications that children needed the innate wickedness beaten out of them. As Amber sniffs and searches, the facts pile up around her in untidy stacks. Hunched over her computer, she recoils at the complacency, at the selective blindness, at the cauterised emotions of those hundreds or maybe thousands of complicit adults. She reads that more than half a million children were institutionalised during the mid-twentieth century. That required a lot of so-called 'carers'. She finds out that these institutions have gradually been closed down and she ponders what happens now? What with all the drugs and domestic violence, the media is constantly reporting individual horror stories of child neglect or abuse. Amber usually ignores these stories. Probably just an odd incident that gets blown out of proportion, but now she wonders. Are there still cover-ups about these unsavoury aspects of a seemingly civilised society?

The newly shaped Amber is headed in a new direction. The abstract theories of art and literature are losing their intrigue and a more pragmatic young woman is emerging into a world not quite as bright and shiny as it once was. She wants to be part of a society that helps children develop into responsible, functioning adults. She wants to make a difference by becoming a teacher. After her Arts degree, that's what she'll do.

Her own childhood was pretty mundane, although she has never been in doubt about being totally cherished and always safe. Her parents divorced and she did the back and forth between houses along with her younger brother. There were some benefits to be had and it didn't take Amber and her brother Troy long to work out how to get double birthday and Christmas presents. Especially from their dad, who played the role of weekend 'good' parent.

Awww. Dad. Mum won't let us have takeaway. Can we have hot chips tonight?

He always gave in. It was a cinch and she and Troy have a laugh about it now. Now Troy's a policeman and really loves the job stationed in a small country town. She did a few years of waitressing and travelling before starting uni. There've been a few longish relationships. She'd thought Kaz might last but it seems to have fizzled out. She's got plenty of time to make choices about partners and whether or not to have children. Or maybe she could choose to have children on her own. Times have changed from the days when a single mother was branded morally contaminating and had her baby forcibly adopted.

Morally fucking contaminating! What the hell is that supposed to mean? And what a joke that is when you find out what really went on behind the locked gates of those children's homes.

Amber's voice is rising and she is scowling at the café patrons who seem to be less angry about life. She's having a coffee with her girlfriend Zoe and after only five minutes she is proselytising again. Her friends are fed up. Where's the fun girl with crazy blue hair?

She charges on despite Zoe's blank face.

Hardly any of those kids were even orphans. Just being illegitimate or having divorced parents was enough to be locked up. Jesus, Zoe. Half of us would have been in homes in those days.

Yeah. Well, I guess people thought they were doing the right thing.

Zoe is only half listening.

The 'right' thing! I so didn't expect you to make excuses for the totally criminal stuff that happened to those kids.

That's it. She's as bad as Storm. Amber is blocking her on Facebook.

Zoe needs to get to her nail appointment. She's going to a hen's party tomorrow night.

Amber has taken it for granted that she is a feminist. But what does that mean? Men don't hold doors open for her, or walk on the outside of a pavement. She goes where she likes without a male to chaperone her. She'll choose her own partner if and when she wishes. Marriage will not be her only pathway into an intimate relationship. She may choose to marry or not, she's never given the issue much thought. Of course, she believes she is equal to any man. Does that make her a feminist or is she just reaping the benefits of those earlier bra-burning outraged women?

She's aware of the way things once were for women. Sad. Terribly sad when she thinks about it more. She understands that gender roles assigned women to marriage and childbearing whether they liked it or not. That they just had to get married because there was obviously something wrong with them if they didn't. That they certainly didn't wait around until their thirties, by which time they were on the shelf – possibly damaged goods or not quite right in the head. She knows all that stuff, but things have changed.

Thank God, because she can't imagine herself so controlled by social mores. Like being a prisoner. How women stayed sane at all is a miracle. Although there were those who didn't, she realised, women who gradually disintegrated as their lives shattered around them. No one to rescue them from loveless, lonely or violent marriages. 'Till death do us part' was a life sentence and even the law could do little, as evidence for divorce was almost impossible for the average woman to substantiate. It makes Amber shudder to think about their powerlessness and the whole patriarchal control thing. She hadn't really realised until she started researching about the kids in homes, that whatever men did behind the closed doors of the family home was sacrosanct. And that professionals like doctors were happy to maintain the status quo by prescribing sedatives for the emotionally weak and sometimes over-excitable housewives. A woman could be black and blue but it wouldn't be noticed. Banging into cupboards and brooms and doors was what women did. They were physically unbalanced as well as unsteady in the mind.

What she's also found out is that if families didn't fit the perfect model of a sober breadwinner as father, a smiling and well-groomed homemaker as mother, accompanied by several, but not too many, well-disciplined, exceptionally clean children, they were deemed deficient. These families did not provide the right influences. An upright society demanded drastic intervention and an institution was the answer.

Amber's initial fury about past injustices has given way to a weary despondency. She begins to acknowledge the dogged determination and tenacity required by those early feminists. By comparison, she feels pathetically soft. It takes the sniff of summer to reinvigorate her. The sun and salty waves are her soul food. Between lectures she bolts to the beach. It's here that her mind shuffles all the information she's crammed in, as she lies drying in the sun.

Kaz wanders up the sand and plonks himself down on the edge of her towel.

Hi, Amber. Wanna coffee?

No thanks. Got uni.

Oh yeah. How's it going?

Okay. I'm doing a Dip Ed this year.

Kaz gazes out at the waves. He's tanned, good-looking, buffed, and Amber feels a momentary sense of lust. Then loss. The moment doesn't last.

Always thought you'd make a good teacher. You're pretty bossy.

She stands up and drags the towel from under him.

Gotta go. I've got assignments to finish. See you, Kaz.

Amber feels renewed by the surf and the brightness of summer. She dyes her hair postbox red to match a gorgeous vintage sun-frock she found at a market. Red and white satin polka dots with a black satin trim. The full skirt shows off her tanned legs and makes her feel sexy again. She's working on an oral presentation for her next class. It's for her History of Education unit. She looks back at some of her research on children's homes and finds an interesting link between institutionalised children and lack of education. She knows that education was mandatory from late in the nineteenth century and wants to find out how these children had been denied the same educational opportunities as others. As she trawls through reports and papers, she discovers the common factor: children were exploited as child labour. What kind of work did kids have to do, she wonders? She discovers that by the age of six or seven most children had to work part or sometimes the whole of every day. All domestic duties and the chores required to run homes, which were often huge old mansions, were assigned to the children. Outside farm, garden, building and maintenance work was for boys and all inside work was for girls. Scrubbing and polishing floors, dusting, washing windows, lighting furnaces and coppers, collecting coke, setting tables, laundry work, cleaning toilets and bathrooms, kitchen work and caring for toddlers were just some of the endless indoor jobs for girls. Many homes ran commercial laundries, which catered for hotels, hospitals and schools. This unpaid labour force proved lucrative for many of the institutions. No wonder there was no time for schooling.

Amber tries to remember what jobs she had to do when she was six. Make her bed, which meant pulling the doona up to the pillow, and feed the dog, which required scooping a cup of biscuits into his bowl. That was as tough as it got until she was a teenager and was expected to help her mum with the dishes and hanging out the washing. Some of her friends did absolutely nothing and still think cooking is heating up a takeaway in the microwave.

She got a great mark for the presentation.

Very well researched and competently delivered. Well done, Amber. You obviously feel passionate about your subject.

Amber had unearthed a quote by Aristotle that she had included in her presentation: *Give me the child until he is 7 and I will show you the man.* She had been astonished that long before the advent of modern psychology, he had recognised those early years as being critical in shaping an adult. She was equally astounded that two millennia later those in charge of children's welfare and protection seemed to have little interest in such ideas. Her classmates had gasped as she'd quoted a former NSW Deputy Premier and Minister for Education from 1956: *Deprived children, whether in their own home or out of them, are a source of social infection as real and serious as are carriers of diphtheria and typhoid.*

These findings fuelled her determination to become a committed and compassionate teacher. Her first love was early childhood education. She'd always related easily to young children and loved their uncensored and quite unique view of the world. *Why have you got blue worms on your legs?* her four-year-old cousin had enquired loudly of Amber's mum at a family picnic. The shorts never came out again after that.

The desire to become an excellent teacher who can make a difference to young children's lives drives her. She graduates with excellent results.

Mum. I've been offered a pre-primary class in Busselton. I'm stoked. It's a new school. I'll be close to the beach. I can get a dog.

You deserve it, Amber. You've worked so hard and I know that you will be a fabulous teacher.

Her mum is congested with pride.

Busselton, the class, the school, the staff: they are all great. Her mum was right. Amber is a fabulous teacher and delights in sharing the wonder and excitement of new discoveries and experiences with her young charges. They literally soak up everything around them and think she is the fountain of all knowledge.

Miss Young said that the moon is not made of cheese. It's dust, Brayden informs his mum as she greets him at the door.

She is in awe of their trust and curiosity and knows she's playing an important part in making their world special. She believes she is making a difference even for these lucky kids with committed parents and beautiful surroundings. There is little want in this middle-class community. Amber hopes that for these children the main threat is over-indulgence. Which may result in some unpleasant traits but not lifelong dysfunction.

Weekends are sometimes wild and always fun. The surf and the beach are as good as it gets. Her shoulder-length hair is now honey blonde. She settles down with a tradie called Jake and they plan a future together.

They buy an old groupie house in Margaret River and start renovating. The jarrah floorboards are stunning once they are polished and Jake's workmanship is brilliant. They move in after only six months.

You must be the couple who have bought old Billy's house. Come over for a drink and meet a few neighbours, says the young woman from a few doors down.

A gathering of young couples like them, some with small children. Amber feels an immediate sense of connection.

Poor old Billy. He had a mental disability. He was in a home as a kid and was abused, I believe. Disgusting the kinds of things that went on. Thank God we don't have places like that any more. Another chardonnay, Amber?

Back in her classroom, she notes that Emily is missing. For more than two weeks. Must be hand-foot and mouth or something, concludes Amber. Yet when Emily returns there is no mention of what has kept her at home. Neither Emily nor her mum say anything. And later when Amber talks to her, Emily's face is a mask, her eyes blank. She mostly plays in the home corner. She wets her pants. She becomes rigid as Amber tries to change them. Amber mentions these changes to Emily's mum Stacey, who is always in a hurry. An attractive woman who wears sunglasses and a cap most of the time.

Things are kind of hectic at our place at the moment. Emily might be overtired, is all she has to offer.

The school term rolls on. Emily is the same. Then she is absent for three weeks. It's her grandmother who drops her off and asks to have a word with Amber in private.

Emily is staying with me for the time being. There have been some family problems, she says.

Emily has become attached to the doll in the dress-up corner and is fretful if another child is playing with it. Today, Amber observes Emily in the sandpit. She has brought the doll outside with her and is stuffing sand into its mouth.

You mustn't tell. It's a secret, she admonishes.

Amber's breath tears at her throat.

Her mind floats away from her body.